# ESCAPE THE PAST

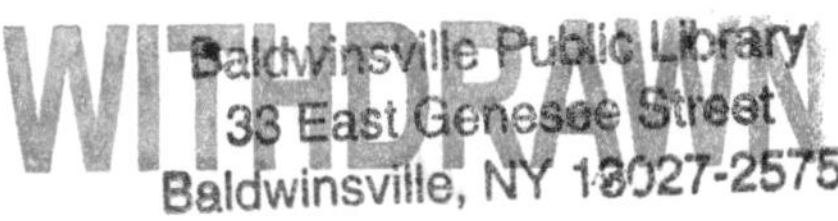


# ESCAPE THE PAST

Patt Parrish

**Thorndike Press • Chivers Press**
**Thorndike, Maine USA Bath, England**

This Large Print edition is published by Thorndike Press, USA and by Chivers Press, England.

Published in 1999 in the U.S. by arrangement with Joyce A. Flaherty.

Published in 1999 in the U.K. by arrangement with the author.

U.S. Hardcover 0-7862-2028-7 (Candlelight Series Edition)
U.K. Hardcover 0-7540-3869-6 (Chivers Large Print)



The text of this Large Print edition is unabridged.
Other aspects of the book may vary from the original edition.

Set in 16 pt. Plantin by Minnie B. Raven.

Printed in the United States on permanent paper.

---

**British Library Cataloguing in Publication Data available**

---

**Library of Congress Cataloging in Publication Data**

Parrish, Patt, 1942–
Escape the past / Patt Parrish.
p. cm.
ISBN 0-7862-2028-7 (lg. print : hc : alk. paper)
1. Large type books. I. Title.
[PS3566.A755E8 1999]
813′.54—dc21 99-27126

# ESCAPE THE PAST

# Chapter One

Elliot Pollock took a deep breath to try to control his rising temper. "Dana, I have too much to take care of this month already. Unless you give me at least one reason for refusing to handle the Ravenel collection, it is your responsibility."

Averting his sharp eyes, she flicked an imaginary piece of lint off her immaculate skirt. Her employer had just stated her problem . . . she couldn't come up with a rational excuse not to do her job. Nor could she tell him how the name of Ravenel made shivers of icy panic run up and down her spine.

Raising her eyes, she stared at the letter he held in his hand. "Do you know who will be arriving to make the arrangements?"

"It doesn't say," he replied. "Just that someone from Ravenel Farms will see us on June 27th. Correction. Will see *you* on June 27th to discuss the exhibit. There is no mention of any particular person."

"June 27th! That's tomorrow!" she gasped.

"Indeed it is." He peered at her through

his horn-rimmed glasses that made him look like a benevolent owl. "And you will handle all the necessary paperwork and take care of anything the Ravenels want done. Right?"

He really didn't expect an answer, which was just as well. All she had been able to say the last fifteen minutes was that she would not deal with the Ravenels. As assistant director of the large tourist shopping center, the Village West, it was part of her job to handle the administrative details for exhibits in the museum. The Ravenel Collection was being offered for a short period of time for display and it was up to her to set a date, coordinate publicity, and make insurance arrangements that satisfied both the owner of the collection and the management of the Village West. It was not difficult. She had done it many times before. But Dana had not had to deal with J. P. Ravenel and she certainly didn't want to start now.

She had just returned from a two-week vacation, and while she had been away a letter was received from Ravenel Farms offering the collection for exhibit. If she had been in her office, she would have sent a reply turning down their offer but Mr. Josef, the museum curator, had decided to accept the collection for their next exhibition.

Dana's secretary had returned the acknowledgment letter and sent the appropriate paperwork to the lenders. Dana could only hope that the D. Donatus at the bottom of the correspondence would mean nothing to J. P. Ravenel. After all, eight years had passed.

Elliot impatiently tapped a pencil on the polished surface of his large walnut desk as he studied the woman who had worked for him for six years, first as his secretary and for the past two years as assistant director. He was obviously puzzled by her attitude. Their ideas and personalities had clashed in the past, which is expected when two people work closely together, but this had been the first time she had flatly refused to take on a project.

She looked younger than twenty-five, although her grey eyes occasionally reflected knowledge of life beyond her years. She was dressed in a white linen skirt and navy blouse with several thin gold chains gleaming against the darker color. Her grey-blonde hair was parted in the middle and tied at the nape of her neck with a slim white scarf, the severe style accentuating her slender throat and high cheekbones. She distractedly brushed a few stray tendrils away from her face.

She raised her eyes to meet Elliott's intent gaze. "May I see the letter?"

He leaned forward to hand it to her. Under the "Ravenel Farms" letterhead were two names: J. P. Ravenel and Sebastion Ravenel. Dana had never met his son but imagined that Sebastion was very much like his father. The letter confirmed the date when a representative of the estate would be at the Village to make the final arrangements for the loan of the collection, and it was signed in a bold but almost illegible script.

The tight feeling of panic eased slightly. At least the letter didn't say J.P. was coming himself. It was just possible whoever arrived wouldn't know her.

Elliott lit one of the foul cigars Dana hated. It was his usual punishment for giving him any difficulty. He was a tall, rangy, casually dressed man who seemed to just let things happen, made no plans for the future because it would take care of itself. His unofficious manner and quick wit gave the impression that he was a man who had been handed everything without ever having to earn it.

Just the opposite was true. Elliott and his wife, Marion, had used the small amount of money they had saved to purchase a run-down, three-story abandoned schoolhouse and had converted it into the most popular tourist attraction in Iowa. The converted school gave the public an attractive and fun place to shop while entertaining them with the different demonstrations and displays they wouldn't see anywhere else.

A puff of pungent smoke made Dana cough and she heard Elliott chuckle in delight before he remarked curiously, "I wonder what the 'Honorable' before Mr. Ravenel's name means?" He paused for another puff on the cigar. "Maybe he's a judge or mayor of a town."

Without thinking and in a voice bitter with memory, Dana answered, "It's a title he gave himself. He was the Justice of the Peace of a small town near Storm Lake for many years but J. P. is also his initials. His name is Joseph P. Ravenel."

Elliott came forward in his chair, completely forgetting his horrible cigar for a moment. "You know him?"

She answered warily, "It was a long time ago."

Elliott was so intrigued by the turn the conversation had taken, he stamped out his cigar in the large glass ashtray on his desk without realizing he was doing it. "Did you get picked up for speeding and have to go in front of the Justice of the Peace?" he asked with a big grin on his face.

Trying to keep her voice light, she forced a laugh as she replied, "Nothing like that. I use to live in the area around Storm Lake."

"Did you really? I never knew that. You are familiar with Ravenel Farms and the Ravenels then?"

That was putting it mildly. She wondered how shocked he would be if he knew J. P. Ravenel was unknowingly the father of her seven-year-old half brother, Terry. She sighed inwardly. Elliott was too curious now, especially after she had stepped out of character and refused to handle the assignment concerning the Ravenel exhibit.

He prodded her. "Then why the big fuss about handling the Ravenel Collection? If you know them, it will make the arrangements all that much easier."

There was no way she could tell him. It was too complicated and too painful. It was her own private hell which she had to keep to herself. Perhaps if she talked with him about the collection, it would make him forget the personal questions.

"Did you know that there are over two hundred pencils in Mr. Ravenel's collection? We will only be exhibiting a small portion of it."

"Pencils! I was under the impression that it was a collection of precious gems." He was astounded as he stared back at her.

Dana couldn't help laughing at the expression on Elliott's face. "I don't know how you got that idea. The collection is described right here on the loan forms." She paused for a moment, then continued with a sarcastic edge creeping into her voice. "I suppose it does sound like an odd hobby for a man with the wealth and property he possesses, but the collection's high market value makes it a natural for the great J. P. Ravenel."

"I take it you are not overly fond of him."

Dana considered her answer carefully, not wanting to give anything away. "J.P. has a way of getting what he wants no matter who is in the way or who he has to step on. He has a large amount of property with orchards as well as farm land. But some of his acreage has been obtained by means that could not be called 'honorable.' He also owns about half the business district of Storm Lake. At least he did years ago. I don't imagine that has changed."

She didn't mention that the collection had once belonged to her own father and to her grandfather before him. Nor did she explain how J.P. had acquired it. The less she thought about her mother's involvement with J.P., the better it was for her peace of mind. Going over the past never changed it. She had worked hard to put the past into a proper perspective and had finally been able to place the bad memories on a shelf in the back of her mind. She didn't need to bring them out again.

Elliott's voice broke into her thoughts. "And this Sebastion Ravenel on the letter-head? Exactly who is he?"

"J.P. has a son. I imagine that's who Sebastion Ravenel is. I never met him. He was away at college when . . . when I lived in the area."

"And the collection?"

Dana took a deep breath, wishing she had never started this. "Years of collecting, re-search, and travel to secure the right pencil had been done before J.P. had even heard of it. Actually, he acquired the collection after it was already compiled. I have no idea if he's added to it in recent years." She shrugged her slim shoulders, not wanting to go into detail about how he had come to possess it in the first place.

Elliott looked doubtful. "Why are these pencils so valuable?"

"There are a number of unusual souvenir pencils, advertisement pencils, and one of the first pencils manufactured in this country . . . that type of thing. There is also a small group of pencils from Germany kept under lock and key. They have an extraordinary history that makes them priceless, and very few people have ever seen them. He may or may not include that group in the public viewing."

Frowning down at her, Elliott stood up and walked over to the window to open it. The cigar smoke was still clinging in the air. He turned around and looked at her strangely. "For someone who didn't want to have anything to do with the Ravenel Collection, you certainly know a lot about it. I still don't understand why you are making such a fuss about handling the arrangements. It sounds like an interesting item for the museum and should draw some extra people to the Village."

"J.P. can . . . be difficult," she stated vaguely. She had always tried to keep her private life separate from her business life. It was one reason why she got along well with Elliott and Marion and she planned to keep it that way.

Getting to her feet, she reached for her linen jacket, which was draped over the back of her chair. "I had better get to work. I'll let you know how things develop with the collection."

She went out the door before Elliott could say another word. He wasn't through discussing the Ravenels but she certainly was.

Even mentioning the name of Ravenel brought back too many painful memories and she could only hope that the transportation and display of the collection could be coordinated quickly and smoothly. Once it was returned to Ravenel Farms, she could go on with her life without being reminded of the man who had destroyed her family.

Several hours later Dana stood leaning against the wooden rail of the third floor balcony looking down into the courtyard below.

The hot midday sun should have tempted the tourists to take advantage of the cooling water in the lake instead of spending their vacation time and money in the shops at the Village West. But here they were in large numbers buying souvenirs and watching the craftspeople demonstrate their various talents.

Several elderly people were sitting on the benches placed along the sidewalk taking advantage of the shade trees bordering the wide walkways. Young children were running in and around groups of shoppers, narrowly missing several package-laden customers. Two impatient children were pushing and shoving each other as they waited their turn at the bubbling drinking fountain.

Dana smiled to herself as she saw a teenage boy tease a girl while they waited in the crowd of people in front of the ice cream parlor. She glanced at the small watch on her wrist. Another ten minutes before the managers' meeting. She straightened and looked in the direction of the lake that she could see in the distance, its surface flickering with silver lights as the sun reflected off the water. The desire to leave work and go for a long swim in the cooling water was almost overpowering. Maybe that would help get rid of this restless, unsettled feeling she had had since the meeting with Elliott. Sighing heavily, she lifted her face so the rays of the hot sun could lay its comforting warmth on her skin.

"It must be nice to spend your working hours standing out here in the sun," a voice spoke behind her.

Dana turned and smiled at the petite woman who had joined her near the rail. "I'm counting customers," she quipped.

Barbara Ealand chuckled. Her short-cropped dark hair and small expressive features blended to give her the appearance of an impish pixie. "Sure you are," she grinned. Looking down at the scene below, she added, "Look at those people. They could be getting sand in their hair and a lovely blistering sunburn but instead they choose to spend their time here."

Dana said drily, "Be glad they do or you and I would be out of a job."

"So speaks the dedicated assistant director. Come on, admit you wish you could join the holiday makers rather than go to the dry old managers' meeting."

Leaning back against the rail, Dana sighed, "You're right. Especially this one. I may have to do battle with Janelle Duvall again unless Elliott feels generous and will take her on."

"Isn't she the new manager of the greeting card shop on the second floor?"

Dana nodded. "She has been there only two weeks and hardly a day goes by since then that she hasn't tried to change some longstanding rule that everyone else accepts. She doesn't like the hours we are open or the type of music on the public stereo system." She smiled down at Barbara. "She wanted classical music only. Said it would draw a better class of people."

Barbara laughed. "What class of people does she expect to get to buy greeting cards?

It seems to me she would want all types of people."

"I finally showed her the survey from the electronics firm which showed what type of music suited the masses and also put people in the right mood to buy before she would give up the idea."

"What do you think she will come up with today?"

Dana brushed a lock of hair back into place. "I hear she has been making inquiries about moving her card shop to the third floor."

Barbara's dark eyes widened in surprise. "She can't be seriously considering putting her card shop in Snob Row?"

"Evidently she does." Dana smiled broadly. "How about you? Do you have any ambitions to move the art gallery from the second floor to the third?"

"You've got to be kidding. The third floor shops sit like high-class potentates condescending to the peasants just by opening their doors and allowing the public to peek at their treasures."

Dana's lips twitched. "I'm on the third floor too, you know."

Barbara grinned, "So you are."

Dana again glanced at her watch. "I suppose we had better go to the conference room. I meant to ask you earlier — are you still planning on a field trip on Sunday?"

They walked along the wooden walkway in the direction of the office as Barbara answered her. "I feel like painting some country scenes. There is one particular barn about ten miles south that is just what I had in mind. How about you? Can you get away?"

Dana opened the door to the offices. "Give me a call Saturday morning. I'll know more then how things are going here and at home."

Barbara nodded as they headed in the direction of the conference room. "Oh, I forgot to tell you. Your painting of Terry was bought this morning. The one where he is wading on the shore of the lake."

"I suppose a woman bought it who has a son his age and it reminded her of her son."

"As a matter of fact it was a man who bought it. A very attractive man at that. He said the boy in the painting looked familiar, almost like himself when he was that age. It does look a little like him." She looked puzzled when Dana stopped abruptly. "He is going to pick up the painting later today."

Dana felt a shiver of apprehension. "Who . . . what's the man's name?"

Barbara looked at her strangely. "I believe

it said Ravenel on his check. Something like that. Why?"

Several managers were coming toward them and Dana gripped Barbara's arm, pulling her in the direction of her own office. Once inside, Dana closed the door and faced a surprised Barbara.

"You will have to give him back his money, Barbara."

"What?" Barbara said in astonishment. "But Dana, why?"

"Just do as I say. Give him back his money and tell him the artist says the painting is not for sale."

"I can't do that. I accepted his check."

"You said the painting is still in the gallery."

"Yes, it is. He had other shopping to do and didn't want to carry it around with him. My assistant was wrapping it when I left to come up here."

Dana indicated the phone with her hand. "Call her and tell her to unwrap it."

Barbara's dark eyes were snapping with temper. "Now, wait a minute, Dana. This is *my* gallery we are talking about. You have put your painting on exhibit and agreed to abide by the sale agreement like any other artist. You can't suddenly decide not to sell a painting which has already been sold. You can withdraw it at any time before that but not once it has been sold."

Dana's dark eyes were hard and determined. "I'll pull rank if I have to, Barbara."

Barbara's face showed her amazement at the change in Dana. "You really would." It was a flat statement but almost sounded like a question as if she wasn't sure she had heard correctly. "I don't have much choice then, do I," uttered Barbara quietly.

Dana's face relaxed slightly. She was about to say something when the buzzer on her desk intruded into the tense atmosphere. She leaned across her desk and depressed the switch. "Yes?"

"Miss Donatus, the managers are all assembled except for Miss Ealand and yourself."

"We will be right there." She turned back to Barbara, a serious expression in her eyes. "Look, Barbara. I'm sorry I had to do it this way. I can't explain why I'm insisting you refuse to sell my painting to this man. As the owner of the gallery, you are right in what you have said, but in this one instance, I'm asking you to give the customer his money back." She paced the floor restlessly in front of the desk. "It's not only myself that is involved or I would explain more. All I can say is that a Ravenel cannot have a painting of Terry."

Dana was trying to soften the command by explaining her actions as far as she could. Because of their friendship, Dana was doing something she didn't usually do, give a reason for an order.

Barbara looked worried. "He isn't going to like this one bit. He appears to be the type of man who likes to have his way."

"I know I've put you in an awkward position but believe me, it's important."

Barbara smiled tentatively, "Well, I can't say it will be good for business to refuse a sale but I'll do it this once."

Dana's smile showed her relief. "Is it still on for the weekend?"

Barbara's humor returned. "Of course. I'll invite several others and we will have a picnic and spend the day painting from dawn to dusk." She started to reach for the phone and added, "You can bring the food."

Dana stood by while Barbara phoned her gallery. She felt as if she had just averted a major disaster . . . which is what it would have been if a Ravenel had taken the painting of Terry. Possibly, just possibly, J.P. would notice a similarity in the boy's features and be curious enough to investigate. She couldn't let that possibility exist.

# Chapter Two

Several hours later Dana was sitting at her desk signing the letters she had dictated earlier. She glanced at her watch. Five o'clock. She buzzed her secretary and asked her to come to her office.

Louise Brynes entered the room and approached the chair in front of the desk. She was a small woman in her early forties, neat and efficient, with reddish-blonde hair cut short. Louise had been Dana's secretary for the past two years, ever since Dana first became assistant director. Louise had never married, preferring her single life. In contrast to her immaculate appearance during the week, the older woman was a camping fanatic, spending her weekends in her large camper van seeking rough, wild terrain. For such a small woman, she handled the big van with ease.

Dana looked up and smiled, "Here are the last of the letters. Is there anything else that has to go out today?"

Louise sat down, kicking off her shoes and reaching for a cigarette all in one motion.

"Nothing that can't wait until tomorrow." This informal ritual was a tradition at the end of each working day.

Dana leaned forward to take a cigarette from the pack out of habit. She frowned. Putting the cigarette back, she rested her head on the high back, resisting the temptation.

Louise watched her. "You look tired."

"It's been quite a day." She raised her eyes to meet Louise's gaze. "What did you think of Janelle Duvall's latest suggestion?"

Louise snorted rudely, "A card shop on the third floor. What next?"

Dana chuckled. "Did you see Elliott's face when she mentioned it? I should have warned him."

"He certainly put her in her place, although for a minute I thought he was going to make you do it. I like the part where he said he had planned the Village so it would offer something for everyone with all types of income and how the third floor was delegated for the higher-income bracket. She didn't like it one bit when he said the card shop just wasn't appropriate."

Dana said drily, "She gave him a good fight anyway."

Louise put out her cigarette in the ashtray before slipping her feet into her shoes. She reached for the letters and walked to the door. As she opened the door she asked, "You don't plan on working late tonight, do you?"

"No. I'm going to change here and go for a swim at City Beach. It shouldn't be too crowded now."

"Why don't you just go home and swim at your own beach?"

"Terry warned me this morning that he was having his friends over to work on the canoe so if I want a peaceful swim, I'd better settle for the City Beach."

Louise laughed, "You mean you don't want to get roped into working on the canoe?"

Dana smiled. "Hopefully the hammering and sawing will be over by the time I get home."

"Well, enjoy your swim. See you in the morning," said Louise over her shoulder.

Dana sat for a moment before pushing her chair back. She went into the adjoining bathroom and started to change into her black bikini. She planned to put her clothes back on until she got to the beach but before she could do that, she heard voices in the reception area. A male voice was loud over Louise's soft tones and it didn't sound like Elliott. Dana walked to the doorway of the bathroom and stood listening. Suddenly her office door burst open and a man entered.

He was majestically tall, well over six feet, barely clearing the doorway as he stopped suddenly just inside the entrance when he saw her. His penetrating dark eyes scanned every inch of her as she stood framed in the doorway.

Dana stared back at the intruder. The resemblance to Terry was unbelievable. He had to be a Ravenel. Was he J.P.'s son? By the angry look in his eyes, he wasn't here for polite conversation. Then she remembered the painting. He must be the one who had wanted to buy the painting of Terry.

When he spoke, his voice was angry. "What kind of business is this? I came here to see the director and instead I find his sexy plaything."

Her secretary rushed in behind him. "I tried to tell this man we were closed for the day but he wouldn't listen."

"It's all right, Louise. You can go. We can't help it if this gentleman is more accustomed to that type of behavior and assumed the worst." She grabbed the skirt and blouse that were hanging on the towel rack.

Louise hesitated. "If you are sure I should leave . . ."

Dana nodded confidently to her secretary. "See you in the morning."

As the door closed behind her, Dana met the intruder's steely gaze. "If you'll wait for one moment, Mr. Ravenel, I'd be happy to discuss your complaint."

A short while later, Dana had emerged from the bathroom fully dressed and was leaning her hip against the front edge of her desk. Feeling more businesslike than she had in the skimpy bikini, she looked the man squarely in the eye.

"How do you know my name?" he asked impatiently. "Were you expecting me?"

"No, but I should have, I suppose."

Her words puzzled him but he disregarded the obscure meaning of her remark. His eyes bored into hers, contempt in their depths. Then he went to the restroom door and looked in briefly before he came back to stand several feet from her. She could see he was keeping a firm control on his temper but she knew she didn't dare push him too far.

"Where is your . . . friend?" he asked nastily.

"Which friend is that?"

"The director. I want something straightened out and I'm not leaving until I do." He reached inside his jacket and withdrew a pack of cigarettes. Dana picked up the lighter on her desk and flicked the button causing a flame to rise. At the sound he looked in her direction. She released the button, extinguishing the flame and tossed the lighter to him. He didn't even look at the lighter as he reached out and caught it, his eyes thoughtful as he continued to study her. He used the lighter and inhaled deeply. His lips twitched in amusement as he tossed the lighter back to her.

As she caught it, she thought it was as if the lighter represented a challenge being tossed and accepted and then returned. She moved around the desk and sat in her chair, setting the lighter back on the desk.

"Please sit down, Mr. Ravenel," she requested quietly, reverting to a businesslike tone, indicating the chair on the other side of her desk. "You want to know why the painting you bought earlier in the day was no longer for sale when you went back to pick it up. Am I right?"

He was surprised and showed it. "How do you know that? Did the owner of the gallery call to warn the director I was on my way up here?"

"She didn't call and I hope you didn't give her a rough time. I'm the one who told her to give you your money back."

She watched his face as he reacted to her

words. She had learned early in dealing with people that the best defense was a strong offense and hoped she could keep him off-balance by surprising him. Looking at him, she didn't think this man would stay off-balance for long. He seemed diabolically self-assured.

"You stopped the sale? Who the hell are you?"

Her voice remained cool. "The artist who painted it, for one thing."

"And for another?" he asked.

"I'm also the assistant director of the Village West."

He had been in the process of putting the cigarette in his mouth but stopped several inches away as she spoke. His eyes narrowed angrily and his voice was harsh. "Pull the other leg, sweetheart. Sexy bikini-clad teenagers do not become directors of a business as big as this one."

"Assistant director," she corrected calmly. She took a cigarette out of the pack. "Look, Mr. Ravenel. I've had a busy day. The office is closed and you probably have other things to do so let's make this quick. The painting is no longer for sale. Your money has been refunded. If you want an apology for any inconvenience, you have it." She stood up in a gesture of dismissal but he wasn't moving. She saw a faint smile cross his features, making him even more attractive.

He was amused. He wasn't reacting like most people did to her authority. But then he apparently still believed she didn't have any authority.

He sat down in the chair she had indicated earlier and looked up at her as she stood at her desk, making her feel foolish. He said coolly, turning her previous words back at her. "Sit down."

She found herself obeying him. She was at a loss as to how to get rid of this arrogant man. Her fingers closed around the lighter as she put the cigarette in her mouth. Then she realized what she was doing and quickly threw the cigarette into the wastebasket. She wasn't going to start smoking again.

He stretched his long legs in front of him and looked relaxed and set for a long chat. "What's your name?" he asked conversationally.

"It was on the door," she responded with belligerence.

"D. Donatus?"

She nodded while she tried to find a way to gain control of the conversation so she could end it.

"You really are the assistant director here?"

Again she nodded.

"But you are just a child." Then he must have remembered the sight of her in the bikini. "Well, maybe not a child," he added with a mocking smile, "but too young for such a position."

"I'm not all that young. I'm twenty-five," said Dana defensively.

"A great age," he commented sarcastically. "What's the 'D.' stand for?"

She tightened her lips into a thin line. "Is that necessary for you to know?"

He shrugged. "Not really." After he had paused to light another cigarette, he repeated, "What's the 'D.' stand for?"

Exasperated and frustrated, Dana answered him. She said her name in a voice that was clearly impatient. It was hard to believe that she was sitting in her office with a member of J.P.'s family several feet away, and feeling nothing but frustration.

She took a deep breath. "I'll show you my credentials if it will help end this conversation."

His lips formed a provoking smile. "I rather enjoyed what you showed me earlier."

His implication was clear and she felt her anger returning, strengthening her. Did all Ravenel men think along the same lines? The picture of J.P. and her mother together on her parents' bed seared through her mind like a hot knife through gauze. Her grey eyes darkened as she looked at him.

"Tell me something, Mr. Ravenel. How are you related to J. P. Ravenel? From your conversation, I have the feeling you are closely related."

His eyes narrowed. "I'm his son. What does that have to do with anything?"

She shrugged, "It makes everything clearer."

"To you maybe but not to me." He stood up — the motion was lithe and graceful for such a tall man — and walked over to the window. His voice was mildly curious as he stared out the window. "Why was I sold the painting this morning and then told this afternoon that someone had made a mistake and my check would have to be returned?"

"The management reserves the right to refuse a sale."

He turned to face her, the light behind him making it difficult for her to see his expression. "Why? Isn't my money good here?"

"You can buy any other painting in the gallery, Mr. Ravenel, but not that particular one."

He crossed his arms across his chest, his voice patient but curious. "Why can't I buy that one?"

He was making her very nervous but she replied calmly, "I have my reasons."

"And my father is part of those reasons."

He wasn't asking a question but she felt compelled to answer, "In a way."

He slowly walked toward the desk, his face expressionless except for his sharp dark eyes. "Since neither my father nor I have been in Clear Lake for a number of years, it must be one hell of a grudge against him. What did he do that carries over to involve me?"

"It doesn't involve you."

His head tilted slightly to one side as he studied her. "You interest me, Dana Donatus. One minute you are a provocative sex kitten in a bikini, then you switch to the cool executive. Now you reveal a vindictive child striking out at me because of something my father did or said that you took exception to." He rubbed his jaw thoughtfully. "What did he do? Make a pass at you?" He smiled cruelly, "Or maybe he didn't make a pass at you. Many women would consider that a worse offense. Which was it?"

Dana felt light-headed with rage. Usually cool and in control of her emotions, it was suddenly frightening to feel this primitive urge to slap that mocking smile off his face.

It would give her the greatest satisfaction to scratch the amusement from his eyes with her fingernails.

The self-discipline of the past rescued her pride before she made a complete fool of herself. Putting a trembling hand to her forehead, she felt the perspiration on her skin caused by the strain she was under to keep her temper. She was unaware of the haunted look in her eyes but the man watching her saw it.

The man watched her as he would a new phenomenon appearing before him in a changing, colorful spectacle. He muttered as if to himself as his eyes remained on her, "You are really something."

His words acted as a douche of cold water on her emotions. She got to her feet using the desk as support, her hands clenched on the surface of the desk. When she was sure her legs would hold her, she walked to the door and opened it. Her voice was strained as she said, "Think what you like, Mr. Ravenel. I couldn't care less. I would like you to leave now."

He slowly stood up and approached the door, stopping near her. A strange tenseness sprang up suddenly between them as he stood close to her. Her mouth went dry and her heart raced when she looked up and saw the disturbing intensity of his eyes as his gaze shifted to her mouth. The air tingled with the sudden sensual tension surrounding them.

His deep velvet voice murmured softly, "Before I go, I want you to know my name is Bass so you can keep me separate from my father." His finger reached out to touch her cheek with the back of a curved forefinger, a trace of mockery in his smile as she flinched at his touch. "Who knows, you may have cause to hate me more than you hate him before we are through with each other."

Dana stared at him. Was he warning her or threatening her?

He moved her hand from the door knob and pulled the door open, closing it quietly but firmly behind him.

The intercom buzzed several times before Dana answered it. It was Louise. "Are you all right?"

"Yes, Louise. I'm fine. Has . . . the gentleman left?"

The older woman sounded disturbed. "Thankfully he left in a better mood than when he arrived. I thought I had better stay in case you needed help. He was quite angry."

"It's been smoothed over, Louise. You go on home now. I'll be leaving shortly."

First she needed a minute to calm down. She was no longer in the mood for swimming. Instead she felt like hitting something. Suddenly it was important to see Terry, to make sure he was there at the cottage. It was a bit silly to feel so threatened — Bass Ravenel couldn't possibly know about Terry — but she did. The more she thought about it, the more she wanted to get home.

She hurried down the stairway until she reached the ground floor and then rushed to her car. Traffic was thick as she headed her car in the direction of the outskirts of town. The cool breeze coming through the open window felt refreshing as the car traveled over the two-lane road that ran along the shore of the lake. It took twenty minutes to reach the cottage, and she finally drove the car up the driveway and parked by the back door.

When she got out of the car, the sound of voices and splashing compelled her to walk around the cottage toward the lake. Terry and several of his friends were swimming near the raft. Towels, rubber floats, and a pair of goggles were scattered on the wooden dock extending out into the lake.

The canoe Terry and his friends were building was perched forlornly on supports while the young construction crew took a break from their labor. Tools were littering the grass around the canoe, wood shavings lying everywhere. Dana sighed. She would have to get after Terry again to make sure he took care of the tools and cleaned up the mess.

She put two fingers in her mouth expertly and whistled a shrill, penetrating whistle as she stood on the sandy beach. She waved when she saw an arm go up in response before he started swimming toward her. Dana's heels struck lightly on the old wood of the dock as she walked to the end, reaching it as Terry grabbed the side to pull himself up a little.

An appealing grin spread across his tan face as he looked up at her. "Hi, Dana. You coming in swimming?"

She smiled. "Not now. You through working on the canoe for today?"

Brushing his wet hair out of his eyes, he nodded. "Billy got a splinter and Freddie hit his thumb so we quit for a while."

"Did you get the splinter out of Billy's finger?"

"Sure. It was just a little one."

Her eyes searched Terry's face looking for the resemblance to Bass Ravenel. She didn't have to look very hard. They both had the same dark eyes and the one-sided smile that could charm the birds out of the trees. She forced herself to be natural with him. "We don't want any serious casualties because of the canoe. You might lose your crew and have to do all the work yourself. And be sure to clean up your mess before you come in."

He pushed himself away from the dock. "I will. We're getting out pretty soon. We're hungry."

"Don't swim any farther than the raft, Terry. You know the rules," she said firmly, trying not to sound too much like an over-protective parent.

He grinned impishly, "I never break rules. You know that."

Dana chuckled. "Only rulers," she murmured as she walked back the length of the dock toward the cottage. She glanced back once to watch him when she got to the beach. He was a good, strong swimmer for a boy his age.

A frown creased her face as she thought of Bass Ravenel and the type of man he was. Would Terry be a copy of the autocratic mold? Terry had never given her any cause to worry concerning his behavior. He rarely rebelled against any reasonable order or discipline. Not that he didn't have spirit. He could assert himself when something was important enough to him.

Dana felt her stomach muscles tighten. What if Terry found out about the Ravenels and the truth of his parentage? There was no way she could gauge what his reaction would be. She could only try to make sure he would never find out. He had accepted the story she had told him about their lack of parents and hadn't asked for any details. As far as she knew, he didn't really mind not having a mother and a father. His sister had always been there. He had never known another way of life.

Edith Parsons smiled at Dana when she entered the kitchen. Edith had been the housekeeper when Dana's family had lived near Storm Lake and was like a member of the family. She not only kept the house sparkling clean but also took care of Terry while Dana was at work during the day. He didn't think he needed a babysitter at his great age of seven but was willing to be under Edith's supervision since he had known her all his life

The older woman continued stirring the batter in the bowl in front of her. "Terry is down at the beach swimming with a few of his friends. They cleaned out the cookie jar, finished the brownies, ate a big bag of chips, and hinted they were still hungry so I'm whipping up a batch of cupcakes."

"I saw the boys when I drove in the driveway," Dana replied absently. How calming this kitchen and this plump comfortable woman were to Dana. All was right in her world as long as this home was intact. The Ravenels were not going to break up this family too.

Edith slid a pan full of cupcakes into the oven and set the timer then poured two cups of coffee and brought them to the table. The two sat opposite each other and enjoyed the casual intimacy of the moment. There was a disturbed look in Edith's eyes as she watched Dana light a cigarette with slightly trembling fingers.

Her voice was quiet as she asked, "I thought you had given them up?"

Dana made a face and stubbed out the cigarette. "I have. It was an automatic thing, I suppose." She threw away the pack she had slipped into her purse at work without even realizing she had done it.

"Did you have a bad day today?"

Dana stared into her cup. "Edith, Bass Ravenel was at the office today."

Edith almost spilled her coffee. "J.P.'s son? Here?"

"I just finished talking to him."

Her face still showing the shock, Edith

asked hesitantly, "He doesn't know about Terry, does he?"

"No." Dana got to her feet and paced the tiled floor. "And he's not going to find out either." She was unable to sit as she told Edith about Bass Ravenel's visit. "He had wanted to buy the painting of Terry from the gallery but I made Barbara refuse to sell it to him. I'm sure he doesn't know who the boy in the painting is but I didn't want him to have it anyway. He exploded into my office demanding to know why he was refused the painting. That's how I met him."

Edith watched her as she nervously walked back and forth in the small kitchen. "Do you think he will be back?"

"This morning Elliott told me to coordinate the exhibit of the pencil collection at the museum. Bass Ravenel may be here to make the arrangements for that." She smiled grimly. "We didn't get around to discussing why he was at the Village today."

Edith sat back in her chair, a deep sigh escaping her. "The pencil collection. After all these years to think the collection is bringing the Ravenels back into your life."

Dana collapsed heavily into her chair. "Ironic, isn't it. That darn collection first brought J.P. to the house years ago." Her eyes were haunted with memories. "Well, he got it, didn't he."

Edith looked at Dana with compassion, knowing the younger woman was reliving the hurt and pain of the past. Her voice was low, "Yes, he got the collection." Her hand came across the table to pat Dana's hand. "Don't think about it anymore, Dana. It's over."

Dana raised her head, her shadowed eyes meeting Edith's concerned gaze. She couldn't tell Edith about the warning or threat that Bass Ravenel had given her just before he had left her office. She wasn't too sure what he had meant, and there was no use upsetting Edith further. He had implied they would be seeing each other in the future. She would make sure it was only one more time and it would be business.

She straightened her shoulders with determination. "I have to see Bass Ravenel or whoever will be delivering the collection, and there should be no reason to have anything to do with them other than a short meeting or two."

She pushed her chair back and went to the sink, emptying the now cold coffee down the drain. She turned around, leaning her hip against the counter. "It's been a long time since I've thought about that day."

Edith said quietly, "I would just as soon

not think of it now."

"I wonder if he ever thinks about it."

"Who? J.P.?"

Dana nodded. "In a way, I'm curious to see how I would feel meeting him again after all this time."

"Dana!" Edith was shocked.

Dana crossed her arms in front of her, smiling faintly without humor. "My reactions wouldn't be as emotional now as they were then, Edith. You don't have to worry about me attacking him again. I was only an immature, sheltered girl of sixteen. I was scared, horrified, and sickened by the things I saw. It was easier to blame J.P. than my mother so I tried to take it out on him."

Edith's forehead was creased with a frown. "Why are you dwelling on it, Dana? You had a difficult time when you found your mother . . . with . . . that man. When your father had his stroke, you were practically on the verge of a breakdown."

Dana took a deep breath. "But I survived And there is Terry. You know, Edith, when I saw Bass Ravenel, I noticed immediately how much Terry resembles him. It's strange how I can love Terry who looks so much like a Ravenel and yet feel such a blinding hate for J.P. and anything connected with him."

"It's not strange at all. That boy is the

only reason you had to keep going." Edith tapped a blunt fingernail against the table top. "What if J.P. arrives at the Village?"

"I doubt if he wants to recall the incident either."

"But if he does meet you again?"

Dan a lifted her chin and answered, "I'll handle the situation as a strictly business transaction. The collection would be the only reason he would be at the Village in the first place. He may not even remember me."

Edith's voice registered doubt. "Will you be able to do that? Keep it strictly business? The last time you saw him . . ."

Dana finished Edith's statement. "The last time I saw J. P. Ravenel, I tried to kill him."

Her words hung in the air as they both sat in silence.

# Chapter Three

The following morning Dana sat at her desk going through some neglected paperwork until the tired muscles in her shoulders reminded her she hadn't moved for a long time. Glancing at her watch, she saw it was already 11:30. She decided to go to the restaurant for a break before the crowd of tourists rushed in for lunch.

At the Brass Rail Restaurant, Dana poured herself a cup of coffee from the large urn behind the counter and slid into the large booth in the far corner of the restaurant where most of the employees congregated during their breaks.

Colby Burris from the pottery shop and Tony Falisco from the woodcarving shop were already seated there and by the number of sketches drawn on napkins and pieces of paper she judged that they had been there for quite some time. Colby, a rather shy young man, gave her a brief greeting and returned his attention to the drawing in front of him but Tony was no longer interested in doodling.

His lip curled into a sneer. “Well, the lofty lady from the top floor has decided to come down among the common folk.”

Dana jerked her head in his direction, surprised at the nasty tone of his voice. Apparently he hadn’t forgotten that incident of several weeks ago.

Ever since he had come to work at the Village about six months ago, Tony had made a nuisance of himself with the female employees. The young attractive ones, of course. At age twenty-one, he had the overwhelming self-confidence that his prettily handsome dark lithe figure was irresistible to anything in a skirt. He had many successes but also a fair amount of failures.

Dana was one of the failures. At first she didn’t take his flirting seriously, but when he began to come on too strong she finally had to put him in his place. Unfortunately this happened in front of several of his friends who were gathered outside the wood carving shop where he worked.

If Tony hadn’t gone too far by lightly slapping her bottom as she was walking by, she doubted if she would have reacted so strongly. She had grabbed a paper cup full of ice cubes and coke held by one of his friends and casually dumped it over Tony’s head as she told him to cool off. His friends had laughed and his handsome face had turned purple with anger and humiliation.

Dana had forgotten all about it but by the look on Tony's face, he hadn't. Ignoring his sarcastic statement, Dana said lightly, "You two seem to be having a working coffee break," indicating the sketches on the table with her hand.

Colby smiled self-consciously but remained silent. Tony leaned back against the cushioned seat and said, "Oh, I like my work, Miss Donatus. But I wouldn't think of jeopardizing my job by taking on more than I should. A person should never try to aim too high in their aspirations for better things."

Dana's voice held a hint of amusement. "If I remember correctly, your problem was that you aimed too low."

His face flushed and he got up quickly and stormed out with a confused Colby left to gather up the sketches quickly and follow.

Dana shook her head briefly. What a fuss he was making. His ego had been bruised by the laughter of his friends but it certainly should have healed by now.

Letting her coffee cool, she looked around at some of the customers in the restaurant. As her eyes roamed over the people seated at the various booths and tables, her wandering gaze met a pair of dark eyes. She and Bass Ravenel stared at each other for a moment. Sitting across from him was the manager of the card shop, Janelle Duvall. It seemed appropriate somehow that the two people who had caused her the most difficulty this week should now be together.

Now was one of the times she wished she hadn't quit smoking. It would have given her hands something to do and conveyed the impression she was relaxed and unconcerned. She knew that he was still looking at her but willed herself to keep her eyes from straying in his direction. Around her she could hear the mumble of voices and the comforting clatter of dishes as business went on as usual in the restaurant.

A few minutes went by as she sipped her coffee, intently watching people entering and leaving the Brass Rail, making sure she never let her eyes meet Bass Ravenel's. Glancing briefly at her watch, she slid out of the booth.

She had just reached the door of the restaurant and was pushing it open when she felt a hand on her arm. Instinctively she knew who it was and attempted to pull away but the grip tightened. She was not-too-gently guided out of the doorway so a woman could pass by.

When Dana turned toward him, her eyes glinted angrily as she met his amused smile. "What do you want?" she asked rudely.

"Miss Duvall suggested you join us for coffee."

Her expression and voice were skeptical. "Did she? Sorry, but I've just had coffee."

His hand released her arm, but she continued to watch him warily. His lean strong body was dressed casually in a grey print shirt open at the collar, and grey slacks accentuated his lean hips and long legs. He radiated arrogance and self-confidence and Dana felt an instant antagonism toward him.

"Is your schedule so full you can't take time for another?" he asked smoothly.

She drew a long deep breath, letting it out slowly as she looked up at him. He waited patiently for her answer. "I can't see why suddenly it is so important for me to have coffee with you and Janelle. I see Janelle almost every day and you have an appointment to see me this afternoon."

His smile was amused. "Did I say it was important?"

She flared up, "Well, since it's not, you'll excuse me," and made a move toward the door only to be stopped by his hand once again. Before she could do or say anything, he had firmly led her to his table and pulled out a chair between his chair and Janelle's.

"I'm so glad you could join us, Miss Donatus."

"My pleasure, Janelle," said Dana with icy sarcasm, rubbing her arm where Bass had held her so tightly. A quick glance at the man on her right showed her that he was thoroughly enjoying himself. She turned her head toward Janelle. "I didn't realize you knew each other."

Janelle smiled sweetly at Bass. "We're old friends, aren't we, darling. We knew one another . . . very well at one time."

While her mind registered just how well they had known each other, Dana murmured, "How nice to renew . . . acquaintances. You two must have so much in common." To begin with, they both had the knack of getting under her skin at every meeting.

A waitress approached the table and Bass ordered a coffee for Dana and refills for himself and Janelle. As the waitress moved away, he commented, "It's not every day I can entertain two lovely women at one time."

Janelle practically purred with pleasure at his words but Dana said drily, "It's little things like this that make life worth living," and saw his mouth twitch at the corners.

The waitress returned with the coffee and placed the cup and saucer in front of Dana. As her arm came into Dana's line of vision, she saw a gauze bandage clumsily wrapped around the girl's arm. "Donna, what's wrong with your arm?"

"Oh, it's nothing much, Miss Donatus. I burned it on the deep-fat fryer."

Ignoring the others at the table, Dana instructed the girl to take off the bandage, which the girl did reluctantly. An angry red welt lay on the girl's forearm. The burn looked serious and extremely painful.

"Have you told the manager about this?" Dana asked the girl.

Donna lowered her eyes. "No."

"Why not?"

Donna's stricken eyes went to the others at the table, as if unwilling to say anything in front of strangers. "I . . . I would be sent home, Miss Donatus."

"You go tell Miss Phillips what happened and show her that arm. She will give you the afternoon off so you can go to the doctor."

"But, Miss Donatus, I . . . you know why . . ."

Dana interrupted, "You take the afternoon off, Donna." She smiled at the girl. "With full pay. Now do as I ask. Miss Phillips will understand. These accidents do happen occasionally."

Donna hesitated, her young tired face showing strain. "With pay?"

"Of course with pay." Then Dana added, "Wear a sweater or long sleeve blouse when you go home. Then your mother won't know it happened. But I insist you see a doctor first." Dana took a pencil and pad from Donna's apron pocket and scribbled a few lines. "Go see this doctor. The Village will pay the bill."

Relief was apparent on the girl's face. "Oh, thank you, Miss Donatus . . . again . . . I haven't been able to repay you for the last time you helped me."

Dana acknowledged her gratitude with a smile and stated firmly, "Get going, Donna. That burn needs attention."

"It . . . does bother me a little."

"I should think so. Don't forget to go to Miss Phillips before you go to the doctor."

As the girl walked away, Janelle remarked, "Your good deed for the day, Miss Donatus? I would think you had enough to do without being the Good Samaritan to the hired help."

Dana's eyes widened at the brittle tone of Janelle's voice but answered calmly by asking a question. "Wouldn't you allow one of your clerks time off if they were injured?"

"Of course but the waitress isn't exactly in your jurisdiction, is she?"

Dana paused, her eyes cold, hating to be put on the spot like this. "Anyone who works at the Village is in my jurisdiction, Janelle." She paused before adding pointedly, "Including managers."

Janelle laughed nervously. "Consider me put in my place, Miss Donatus." She turned to Bass who had been watching the proceedings with interest. "Miss Donatus always has an answer to everything."

Bass was leaning back in his chair watching Dana lazily as if she was the afternoon's entertainment. He smiled crookedly, "So I've noticed."

To Dana, Janelle said too lightly, "That girl seems to have more pull with you than . . . others."

"What is that supposed to mean?"

"Well, you seem to be aware of her problems and you bend the rules for her."

"I don't see where I've bent any rules. She needed medical attention and I insisted she get it. Miss Phillips would do the same if she were aware of the girl's injury. The same is done for any employee at the Village. As a manager, you are fully aware of the policy."

Janelle shrugged her shoulders delicately.

"Maybe I should have said I feel your priorities are strange. A waitress gets more personal attention than a manager."

Dana knew Janelle was referring to their past disagreements. She replied tightly, "Maybe I feel a young girl who is the sole support of a neurotic mother and a deaf brother deserves a bit of extra attention." She glanced at her watch. "Now if you will excuse me, I must get back to the office."

She pushed back her chair and was startled when Bass stood up with her and said, "I'll come with you."

A sound of disappointment came from Janelle. Dana stood behind her chair and met Bass's gaze. "That isn't necessary, Mr. Ravenel. There is no need for you to leave Janelle on her own. Our appointment isn't until this afternoon."

He ignored her, picking up his jacket off the back of his chair. He flung some money down on the surface of the table and gestured that she lead the way.

Exasperated, Dana turned toward the door. After a few words to Janelle which Dana didn't hear, he followed her out of the restaurant. When they reached the office door, he reached over her head and pushed the door open and she entered under his extended arm.

Louise looked up from her desk and was plainly surprised to see who was with Dana. She kept glancing at him as she told Dana of several calls that were waiting for her attention.

"There is a calamity in the Herb Garden Shop. Mr. Pryor found an insect of some kind and wants an exterminator. Mr. Pollock is out of the office for several hours and Mr. Pryor says it is an emergency."

"I'll see to it," Dana said, and picked up the slip of paper on Louise's desk. She went into her office and knew Bass would follow her. She sat behind the security of her desk and reached for the phone. Bass walked to the window, which overlooked the rear of the shopping complex. There wasn't much of a view unless he liked to look at parking lots but he appeared to be fascinated by it.

During the conversation with the manager of the Herb Garden, Dana was very much aware of the man at the window. It was as if a current was flowing from him attracting her like steel filings toward a powerful magnet. She had no idea why he had insisted on coming back to her office now rather than waiting until their appointment. She wasn't too sure she wanted to know.

Bass was still standing by the window when she finally put the phone down after contacting an extermination company but now he was facing her, his back to the window, his expression unreadable. He came toward her desk and sat down in the chair he had occupied during his previous visit. In a businesslike voice he said "Well, Miss Donatus, I believe I am supposed to meet with you to discuss the arrangements for the pencil collection. Let's get that part over with."

She frowned. He made it sound as if there was something else to discuss. "You have an appointment at two o'clock."

"Does it really matter when as long as it gets done?"

"I suppose not," she said wearily with a distinctly unenthusiastic tone.

For the next fifteen minutes Dana went over the specifics of how the collection would be displayed and arranged for a convenient time of delivery. Bass was matter-of-fact throughout the whole discussion. Dana relaxed a little, deciding he just wanted to get the business out of the way so he could do something else in the afternoon.

Finally when all the questions regarding the collection had been answered, Dana had to ask about the one thing that had been uppermost in her mind since she had first seen Bass Ravenel.

"Is J.P. with you?"

Bass looked up from the papers he was reading, puzzled by her question. "My father isn't well. That's why he asked me to handle the disposition of the collection in the first place. He wants to come for the opening day but the decision is in his doctor's hands. Why? I got the impression you didn't care for my father. Or was I mistaken?"

She gave him a resentful look. "Just curious."

The last paper was signed and Bass handed it to her. "I'm surprised you agreed to have the collection on display feeling like you do about my father."

"I was on vacation when the request came. My secretary sent the reply to your father after it was approved by Mr. Pollock."

"If you had been in the office, the reply would have been a polite refusal." It was a statement rather than a question.

She agreed rather bluntly, "Polite or not, it would have been turned down."

He was silent for a long, uncomfortable moment as he studied Dana through narrowed eyes. Then he said, "If the doctor approves, J.P. wants to bring the main part of the collection himself."

"The Commandment pencils?"

He came forward in his chair. "How did you know about them?"

The color drained from her face as she realized her mistake. "You mentioned them," she murmured lamely.

"No, I didn't." His eyes drilled into hers. "What do you know about the Commandment pencils?"

Her voice was shaky as she answered, "Just that there are nine pencils with a Commandment printed on each one."

"Ten pencils, not nine."

It was Dana's turn to be surprised. "Ten! But there can't be. I . . ."

She sat back heavily in her chair. How could there be ten pencils? She had destroyed one herself. In a rage she had taken the pencil with the Commandment, "Thou Shalt Not Commit Adultery" and snapped it in half, throwing the two pieces in J.P.'s face. What was going on? How could J.P. have the tenth pencil? She was almost certain it had been splintered beyond repair.

Dana felt like a tightrope walker after a bad fall, wanting to go on but not wanting to take the first step. There were questions she wanted to ask but a part of her really didn't want the answers. She ran her tongue over her dry lips unaware of the dark eyes that followed her every move. In fact she had almost forgotten he was even there, she had been so deep in thought.

His voice was hard and gritty. "I don't suppose you would be willing to tell me what this is all about? I've never even heard of you but yet you know so much about my father and the collection."

She controlled her expression with a great deal of effort. "No, I wouldn't be willing to discuss anything to do with your father, Mr. Ravenel." Her eyes were clouded, as if hiding unpleasant memories like a soldier who had done battle but didn't want to think of his wounds.

"Maybe I should ask my father since you don't want to provide any answers."

She met his gaze. "It wouldn't affect you even if you knew so why not just leave it alone?"

He took a cigarette out of his pocket. "I'm curious to know what my father has been up to in his murky past." He reached across the desk for her lighter and put the flame to his cigarette, inhaling deeply as he continued to watch her. "Would he tell me or is it too awful to tell?" he asked with sarcasm.

Dana stood up and walked to the window, her back turned toward him in an attempt to shield herself from his hostility. She spoke flatly, "I don't imagine your father even remembers me, Mr. Ravenel. He met me only once."

She heard the chair move against the carpet and turned around. Bass had gotten to his feet and was placing the lighter on the desk. He then leaned back. "That must have been one hell of a meeting."

Her expression showed the strain she was under but she didn't speak.

He persevered, "That one meeting had quite an impact on you to hate him so strongly and for so long."

Dana tilted her head to one side as she asked, "How well do you know your father, Mr. Ravenel?"

His mouth tightened as she changed the subject again. "As well as any person knows a parent, I suppose. I was away from Storm Lake for about six years but I kept in touch with him. When he had a stroke three years ago, I came home to take over the farm."

Keeping the conversation away from herself was her main objective as she inquired, "What did you do during those six years you were away?"

"You ask a lot of questions for someone who refuses to answer any."

She smiled faintly, assuming a nonchalance she didn't feel. "You don't have to answer them."

"No, I don't. But if I answer your questions, you just might get the idea how it's done and answer a few of mine." He was still leaning against the desk, looking directly at her as he continued. "I spent four years in college and earned a degree in chemistry, then went to work for a company in England. When I was notified that my father was seriously ill, I went home. There is a laboratory in one of the buildings on the farm, where I work whenever time permits. Being the only son, I have certain obligations to my father and to the estate."

His words struck her like an explosion. He wasn't an only son. There was Terry. For years she had let her hate and disgust for J.P. persuade her she had done the right thing in keeping Terry's existence from the Ravenels. But had she been fair? Would it make a difference to the man sitting on her desk to know his father had another son?

Dana rubbed her forehead and bit her lip, a grave look on her expressive face. For years she had believed that her decision to keep Terry affected only the two of them. Now she realized for the first time that her actions affected not only J.P. but his oldest son. What could she do about it now? What could it accomplish if she told Bass or J.P.

about Terry? She might lose Terry to the Ravenels and she knew she couldn't risk that. What was the right thing to do?

She had been lost in her thoughts for so long that Bass was getting impatient with her silence.

"Remember me?" he challenged.

Startled, she almost jumped when his voice interrupted her tortured thoughts. "Sorry. What did you say?"

His smile was unpleasant. "I haven't said anything in the last few minutes. If my conversation is so boring, you shouldn't have asked the questions." When he didn't get any response from her, he continued, "Look, I don't know what in hell this is all about but I warn you I intend to find out. It's your turn to answer some questions. When did you meet my father?"

Dana took a deep breath and looked at her hands clenched in front of her. She answered guardedly, "Eight years ago."

He hadn't really expected her to answer and when she did he was surprised but persistent. "Eight years ago? What happened?"

"I can't tell you."

"Why not?"

Her voice rose in pitch. "Because I can't."

He came away from the desk and took

hold of her arms in a cruel grip. "What did he do to you?"

"Nothing."

His grip tightened. "He had to do or say something. No one hates someone for so long without a good reason."

Dana tried to squirm out of his hold but her struggles only forced him to hold her tighter, closer. When her slender body touched his, she heard his quick intake of breath and raised her head to look at him. Her hands were pinned against his chest and she could feel his heart beating fast against her finger tips. She was finding it difficult to breathe and trembled violently.

His eyes darkened as he looked down at her parted lips, his hands moving of their own accord down her back as she was pressed into him. She looked away from his blazing dark eyes but she couldn't shut out the male scent of his body or the sensual awareness that had suddenly sprung up between them.

This couldn't be happening. She couldn't be wanting this man to kiss her. He was a Ravenel. Her mouth shaped the word "No" but she never got a chance to speak before his mouth closed over hers in a hungry demanding kiss that rocked her senses. She was drowning in a sea of feelings she had never experienced before, but a part of her held back, refusing to acknowledge the pleasure his nearness gave her.

Suddenly he violently shoved her away from him. Her arm banged into the corner of the file cabinet as she flung it out to keep her balance. Rubbing the bruised area, she looked at him warily.

His hands were shaking as he put a cigarette into his mouth and flicked his lighter. He was affected by her as much as she was by him! He stood still for several tense minutes, silhouetted against the sunlight streaming in the window. She felt slightly nauseous with tension but could only stand there looking at him.

When he turned to face her, his voice was again cool and controlled. "Who is the boy in the painting?"

Her face lost all color as she continued to stare at him with wide frightened eyes. She whispered hoarsely, "Why do you want to know?"

He took several steps toward her, his eyes flashing angrily but he stopped abruptly several feet away. "If you don't stop answering a question with another question, I won't be responsible for my actions."

She swallowed with difficulty. "He's . . . my brother."

That wasn't the answer he had expected. "Your brother?"

"Now that I've answered your question, will you leave my office?"

He ignored her request and again sat on the edge of the desk, his eyes thoughtful and serious.

Dana put her hand to her forehead to try to erase the tension headache beating stronger by the minute. She wanted him to go away. She couldn't cope with any more probing questions. She had the sinking feeling she had given away too much already. In a panic, before she said anything more, she decided she would leave her office since he wouldn't.

Her hand was on the latch of the door when he grabbed her wrist. "Where do you think you are going?"

"Away from you."

He pulled her away from the door and his touch released her pent up feelings. Anger hardened her voice as she practically shouted at him. "Mr. Ravenel, this may come as a great surprise to you but what I do, who I am, and who I hate is none of your business. I am going to tell you about myself just so you will be satisfied and will leave me alone. I am twenty-five years old with a good job which I would like to get back to instead of wasting my time arguing with you. I have a brother and a housekeeper who live with me. I drive a two-year-old car and I paint when I get the time, I'm in reasonably good health, and I detest arrogant men who use their strength to push me around."

She stopped for a breath before rushing on, "I live in a cottage on the North Shore, my teeth are my own, and I like an occasional glass of wine and Chinese food. Now you know everything about me so you can go now."

His smile was full of charm mixed with amusement. "I learned something else. I should have made you angry an hour ago. It would have saved a lot of time. It's one way to get you to talk."

Dana clenched her fists. He looked cool and relaxed while she was trembling with rage. He thought this was just an amusing game.

To make it worse he continued calmly, "There are still some things I don't understand."

She laughed harshly, "You are so right. You don't understand anything." Controlling her temper, she said tightly, "Let it be."

"I don't like unsolved mysteries."

"Well, Sherlock, consider this case closed."

The change in his face should have warned her but she went on sarcastically and bitterly. "The arrogant Ravenels. Demand and everyone has to obey. Well, not me, Mr. Bass Ravenel. So try your caveman tactics on someone else."

His eyes blazed. "Dana, I'm warning you. Be careful how you talk to me."

"Now a threat. Good. We're progressing nicely. It's just like having a conversation with your father. First a nice threat followed by an offer of money. That's next, isn't it?"

She cried out as he grabbed her wrist in a painful grip once again. She was frightened now. He was furious, more angry than she had ever seen anyone. She pleaded with herself not to cry.

She gasped, "Bass, you're hurting me," not realizing she had used his name.

He saw the tears, which she could no longer suppress, and slowly loosened his hold on her as he took a step back. She watched his face change from furious to unreadable. He cursed softly under his breath. Then he said in a controlled tone, "I had better leave before I do something we will both regret."

He moved her aside and opened the door. "I'll be back." Then he walked away.

# Chapter Four

The following day Dana was in her office which was operating at is normal hectic pace. Louise was busy with the piles of paperwork on her desk and the phones were ringing continually. Elliott was yelling into the telephone most of the morning or shouting for his secretary. He had a button on his phone that would summon her but he always preferred to exercise his lungs.

Dana had her share of work to get through. There were letters to be written and signed. People to contact. Complaints to answer. Compliments to acknowledge. Business as usual.

Occasionally the scene with Bass Ravenel intruded into her thoughts but she pushed it back and continued with her work. She had spent a practically sleepless night going over their stormy encounter and had been forced to use more makeup than usual in the morning to cover the dark circles under her eyes. Since she didn't want any questions about the dark bruises on her arm, she wore a long-sleeve shirt to cover them.

During the long night she had tried to remember exactly what she had said to Bass that might enable him to start fitting the pieces together of a puzzle she didn't want him to complete. She had felt frightened enough at one point to hunt for her suitcases but stopped herself before she actually packed anything. To uproot Terry from his school and his friends was a drastic step and wouldn't really solve the problem. If she was right in her assessment of Bass Ravenel, he would follow her. He had said he didn't like unsolved mysteries and he was particularly eager to get to the bottom of this one since it involved his father.

She would have to stay and protect Terry from anything the Ravenels might do when they found out about him. Perhaps if she was careful they wouldn't ever learn the truth of his parentage

A little after two o'clock, Louise buzzed Dana to say she was wanted in the museum. Dana was about to leave her office when Elliott returned from lunch.

He stopped to talk to her. "Where are you headed? Late lunch?"

"To the museum. They just called."

Elliott grinned. "Ah, the famous pencil collection has arrived. I must go see this myself." He yelled at Louise to tell her to tell his secretary where he was going before he opened the door for Dana.

"The collection is here already?" asked Dana as she went through the opened door.

"J. P. Ravenel himself called me this morning and said the collection would arrive this afternoon by messenger. Except the main part which he will bring himself."

Trying to hide the sinking feeling Elliott's words had caused, Dana asked haltingly, "He's coming here?"

Elliott stopped walking, his gaze inquisitive. He lightly touched her shoulder and Dana turned to look at him. He was more perceptive than she had expected. He knew something was bothering her and that it had to do with the Ravenels. She knew that, though Elliott was curious, he wouldn't pry into her private affairs . . . unless, of course, she felt like telling him.

Before he could say anything, she smiled brilliantly and pretended she didn't have a care in the world as she quickly changed the subject.

Once they were in the museum, they headed for the back room where all the deliveries were unpacked and catalogued. Several workmen and the curator were all looking, with somewhat skeptical expressions, into a small wooden crate on a table.

The curator, Mr. Josef, a short, dapper man full of self-importance, seemed to be having second thoughts about whether or not he considered this collection truly worthy to be included in such elite company as original paintings and priceless sculpture. He turned to Dana for confirmation that the pencils were worth displaying.

"Miss Donatus, I am rather startled by the mundane appearance of this collection. I was led to believe that these were rare and extraordinary pencils Mr. Ravenel had gathered in his years of duty on the judicial bench."

An arched brow raised as Dana queried, "Judicial bench?"

Mr. Josef lifted his chin and nose even higher than usual and stated firmly, "Mr. Ravenel personally contacted me to instruct me on the proper way to show his collection to its best advantage. I assured him we would do it justice. He mentioned they had historic value, as well as monetary value. I was quite impressed with Mr. Ravenel's manner."

"I'm sure you were. He meant you to be. That's his way," replied Dana. "You should see him in person . . . aristocratic features, tall, and gives a definite impression of wealth and authority." She didn't mention that J.P. had never been a judge. She would let Mr. Josef have his illusions.

While she had been talking to Mr. Josef, Elliott had gone to the crate on the table and was picking through the contents. "Hey, Dana. Come here and look at this."

He held up a package of pencils encased in a plastic bag with a tag attached. Then he reached into the crate again and brought out several similar packages.

When she reached for the first package, she immediately noticed J.P. had left the pencils in the same plastic cases her father had used for them. All that was different was the wording on the tags and the small print: "Property of J. P. Ravenel."

Between Elliott bringing out cases and Mr. Josef and his assistants doing the same, the table began to overflow with small mounds of pencils. There were round ones, square ones, flat ones. Pencils made of paper instead of wood, spirally-wound and glued at one end. Dana's father had instructed her on how to sharpen this pencil by unwinding the paper as many turns as necessary.

There was a pencil with square lead dated before 1876 when round leads in the center section were first introduced. A drawing of the first pencil made in 1564 when pure graphite was discovered in a mine in Borrowdale, England illustrated how shepherds used crude slabs of graphite wrapped with cord. The crude pencils became popular and were then sold in cities.

There was also a sketch of the first manufactured wooden pencil made in Niirberg, Bavaria in 1662. It showed strips of graphite between strips of wood. There was even an explanation of the method of refining graphite by mixing it with clay which was discovered by Nicolas Jacques Conté, a French scientist and mechanical genius, along with Josef Hardmuth of Austria between 1790 and 1795.

Elliott held a small package with a stub of pencil about two inches long of unfinished cedar, unpolished, very thin, with a square lead. The label read: "This pencil was believed to be one of the pencils manufactured in the United States by William Monroe, a cabinet maker in Concord, Massachusetts. An enterprising dealer, Benjamin Adams, contracted with Monroe to buy all the pencils like this one that he could manufacture."

Elliott chuckled as he regarded the length of the pencil. "This one seems to have been well used."

An example of Joseph Dixon's first round

rather than square cross-section of lead which was introduced in 1876 in Salem, Massachusetts was also included, as well as a sample of the first varnished pencil introduced by George Rowney of Britain.

Elliott's enthusiasm helped to convince Mr. Josef that the pencils might be worthy of his museum after all. He made a point of saying the most important set in the collection would be delivered personally by the owner.

Elliott turned to Dana and inquired, "You know about the collection, Dana. Tell us why those particular pencils are so special."

His voice brought her back from the haunting picture of her father sitting at a table in his study sorting and tagging his various pencils, holding each one gently, a look of pride and possession on his face.

She cleared her throat and explained, "The most valuable part of the collection consists of nine pencils with a Commandment on each."

Mr. Josef responded importantly, "Mr. Ravenel stated there were ten Commandment pencils."

First Bass and now Mr. Josef were insisting there were ten pencils instead of nine. Dana was not about to argue the point but she made a promise to herself to inspect the pencil she knew had been ruined.

Instead she said quietly, "Then the collection is worth a great deal of money."

Elliott was stunned. "Really? It's surprising how little pencils could be worth so much."

She nodded. "The Commandment pencils were believed to have been made by the German Lutheran immigrants who were driven out of their homeland by the Prince-Bishop of the Roman Catholic Church. These Lutheran fugitives founded Lutheran congregations in America in the early 1700s. I don't remember where they settled. When the pencils arrive you will be able to see the Commandment printed on each one which was made by a burning tool of some kind. The words are all in German."

All sorting had stopped as Dana spoke and the faces of Mr. Josef, Elliott, and everyone else in the room showed interest in what she was saying.

One of the assistants murmured absently, "I don't think I'll ever take a pencil for granted again. Look at this one." He held up a package with a stub of pencil inside and read the tag. "Nicolas Jacques Conté was commissioned by Napoleon Bonaparte to develop a substitute for the pencils previously used when warfare cut off all imports to France."

It was now clear that in Mr. Josef's estimation, the pencil collection was of enough importance to be displayed in his museum since he put great store in historical value, although not as much as on monetary value. He turned to Dana. "Will there be adequate security, Miss Donatus?"

"There will be the usual: one guard during the day and another at night. The collection will be in the locked glass cases and the Commandment pencils will be in the special glass case where the Freboli emerald collection was placed last month. The alarm system case. You will have one key and the other will be in my possession. Once the display is in the case, the alarm system will be turned on and will not be unlocked until after the two-week exhibit has ended."

Mr. Josef asked unnecessarily, since he already knew the answer. "And insurance?"

Dana replied patiently, "The usual coverage protecting the museum in case of fire, theft, or vandalism and full coverage for the collection. Mr. Ravenel's son is aware of this and has agreed to these conditions."

Mr. Josef seemed satisfied and went back to the collection.

Dana was deep in thought as she made her way back to her office. Mr. Josef was content with the display but she wasn't. The existence of that extra pencil kept niggling her. She had ruined that pencil. She was positive of that. How could it be included in the collection?

Had J.P. substituted a fake pencil for the real one? If that were true, it would be up to her as the assistant director to report it to Mr. Josef and Elliott. But then she would have to explain how she knew it was a phoney.

On Thursday Marion Pollock came to the office and asked Dana to lunch since Elliott was tied up in a meeting. For a change of scenery and because Dana didn't want to take the chance of running into Bass Ravenel again, she suggested they try a new restaurant downtown rather than go to the Brass Rail Restaurant as they usually did.

After they were seated at a table, Marion entertained Dana with descriptions of the various antics of the Pollock children.

Marion was a natural storyteller. In fact, Marion was good at everything. She was highly organized and her home reflected her ordered style of housekeeping. Every meal was planned in advance, with the menus written down a week at a time.

In her appearance, Marion was as immaculate as her home. Every hair was in place, her makeup was always perfect, her clothing never creased, wrinkled, or showed any signs of grubby little children's hands.

Occasionally Dana wished she could find just one thing Marion didn't do well. It is one thing to put up with a friend's faults but quite another to accept their perfection.

After lunch they were drinking coffee when Marion suddenly became serious as she asked Dana if she felt well. "Is that husband of mine working you too hard? You look like you could use a good night's sleep."

The effects of a couple of restless nights had left their mark. Her normally bright eyes were dull with fatigue and worry and she knew she hadn't made the most intelligent contributions to their conversations. Her nerves were stretched too tightly, making it difficult to sit calmly under Marion's inquisitive eyes.

"I've been having trouble sleeping. That's all."

Marion smiled gently. "That sounds like a man is involved."

A slight tint of color and Dana's startled look gave her away but she denied that a man was the cause of her sleepless nights. She had the feeling Marion didn't believe her and was grateful when her friend left it alone.

"You know Elliott and I are around if you

need any help with anything. I can't suggest a vacation since you just had one but I can suggest you take it a little easier at work." She grinned. "I realize better than anyone that Elliott can be a walking dynamo and expects everyone else to keep up with him. It's not Terry, is it? He is all right?"

Dana smiled tentatively. "He's fine. It's just one of those things that will straighten itself out eventually."

Marion sat back in her chair and asked Dana to tell her about the trip they had taken for their vacation. The rest of the luncheon went smoothly.

That evening Colby Burris came over to spend a couple of hours with Terry, helping him put together a model ship that was too detailed for Terry to work on alone. Colby was twenty years old but mentally slower than others of his age and seemed to enjoy spending time with Terry doing things the younger boys liked to do.

Edith had felt sorry for the shy young man at a Village picnic several years ago and occasionally asked him to come to the cottage for meals. He was at ease with Edith and Terry but seemed uncomfortable around Dana. She had tried to make him feel at home since Terry liked to work on projects that Dana didn't have time to help him with, and she didn't really understand his wariness of her.

This evening she was especially glad Colby was there to keep Edith and Terry occupied and to distract her from thinking of Bass, J.P., and Terry. She felt great pressure as the only one who knew their relationship to each other.

Colby and Terry eventually left the living room to work on the model and all was quiet. Edith was crocheting and Dana was attempting to read a book when the silence was broken by the shrill ring of the telephone.

Terry came bounding out of his room to answer the phone, saying hello breathlessly. With a shrug, he handed the phone to Dana.

She took the phone from his small hand and heard Bass's deep voice on the line. Without making any polite conversation, he got right to the point. "Dana, I wanted to let you know that J.P. will be arriving at the Village tomorrow with the main part of the collection ."

It took her a moment to get over her surprise that he was calling her. "Why are you telling me?"

"I decided I should warn you," he said quietly.

"I see."

"I doubt if you do but I'll let that go for now. I'm not warning you only for your sake. My father has a bad heart and if you saw him unexpectedly, you might say or do something to shock him. I've gathered he is not exactly your favorite person."

Dana closed her eyes for a moment, strangely appalled at the opinion he had of her. "Then you are warning me in more ways than one," she said gravely.

His voice became impatient. "Dana, stop it! Let's not start arguing again. I don't know why we react this way to each other but I don't enjoy it. How about a truce? Whether you believe me or not, I did phone you for your sake as well as my father's, so you could be halfway prepared for his arrival."

His words disarmed her. She hadn't liked the unpleasant arguments either and was more than willing to end them for the short time Bass would remain in Clear Lake.

"I do appreciate you calling," she replied soberly.

"That is a step in the right direction anyway." There was a pause on his end of the phone before he said, "I don't wish to shatter our recent truce so quickly but I have to know." Again there was a brief silence. "Should I also prepare my father for his meeting you?"

Dana sighed, "As I told you before, I doubt if he will even remember me, so it won't be necessary to say anything."

"I'm not so sure he could have forgotten you so easily. You aren't exactly someone who would be easy to overlook."

She smiled slightly, "At sixteen, I was quite forgettable, believe me."

He chuckled before saying, "I'm going to hang up before we start disagreeing again. I'll see you tomorrow."

"Goodbye, Bass."

She heard the click on the line and slowly placed the receiver back on the phone. She turned and saw that Edith had forgotten her crocheting and was watching her.

Edith stated soberly, "It was him, wasn't it?"

Dana approached her chair and sank into it. "It was Bass Ravenel, if that's what you mean. He wanted to let me know his father will be at the Village tomorrow."

Edith's expression was apprehensive. "I didn't realize you were on a first name basis with Bass Ravenel. I thought you had only met him that once."

"He came to the office yesterday to finalize the arrangements for the pencil collection. We argued rather heatedly and somehow started using first names as we shouted at each other."

"Good heavens! What were you shouting about?"

Dana picked up her book from the table and answered, "For one thing he said there were ten Commandment pencils and when I stated there were nine, he wanted to know how I knew about the Commandment pencils in the first place and it sort of got out of hand from then on." She made an impatient gesture with her hand. "It's too complicated to explain. We just seem to strike a wrong chord every time we talk."

"But how can there be ten pencils? I thought . . ."

Dana shut her book and got up to place it in the bookcase against the wall. "I don't understand it either. I'm positive I destroyed that pencil that day." A frown appeared on her lovely face. "I *know* I did, but I can't remember what happened to the pieces." She looked at Edith. "Do you remember seeing them after J.P. left the house?"

Edith shook her head. "There was so much going on that day. When I came back from my sister's, it was such a shock to discover your father had passed away. Your mother was crying and you, well, you were . . ."

Dana's smile was full of self-derision. "Upset? Looking back now I realize how childishly I behaved but my whole world had turned upside down."

Edith was thoughtful, and there was a hint of sadness in her voice. "When I left the house on Saturday, you were a carefree teenager full of laughter and devilment. When I returned on Sunday evening, you were full of hate with a promise in your eyes to remember that day."

Dana sat down in her chair and stared at nothing, seeing the scene in her mind as if it were yesterday. "I remember feeling young and inadequate when I rode in the ambulance with my father. I was completely helpless the whole time I remained with him." Her voice was husky with remembered pain. "His last words to me were 'Don't lose your pretty smile.' I didn't feel like smiling when I came home from the hospital and found J.P. still there."

She stood up and went over to the cabinet against the wall and poured two glasses of brandy. She handed one to Edith and they each took a small sip. Dana continued, "I realize how awful I was to mother but she was so self-righteous. Saying over and over that things happen between a woman and a man that I was too young to understand. She said personal things about her life with my father that I couldn't bear to hear. She kept telling me to be reasonable."

She snorted disrespectfully. "I remember asking her why she had always quoted those motherly words of wisdom to me . . . 'Dana, don't let a boy put his hands anywhere below your waist or on your breasts.' 'Dana, you must be a good girl.' When I asked her that night why she had told me all that guff about proper behavior and added, 'Didn't you want me to have fun like you do?', she slapped me."

Dana took another sip of brandy. "I can't say I didn't deserve it but it just fired off my temper. Then J.P. walked into the room holding the case of Commandment pencils. While my father was lying dead in the hospital, J.P. was cold-bloodedly going through the collection."

Edith said softly, "This is the first time you've really talked about that day in years . . . since your mother left us."

Staring down at the amber liquid in the glass, Dana said "Maybe it's time I put it all into its proper perspective, since I will be seeing J.P. tomorrow. I'm older now and hopefully wiser." Her smile was rueful as she looked at Edith. "I shall show great strength of character by not throwing anything at him or attempting to bash him over the head."

"At least you can joke about it now."

Dana's voice was quiet. "My father said not to lose my smile. I should have remembered that sooner. I may need a sense of humor before this is all over."

# Chapter Five

After the first good night's sleep in what seemed a very long time, Dana needed a long shower. Relaxed by the brandy the previous night, she had slept deeply and dreamlessly and needed the blast of cool water to wake her fully.

She wrapped a large fluffy towel around her and went into her bedroom. The house was quiet except for occasional kitchen noises which meant Edith was up also. Dana went to the open window of her bedroom and watched the early morning sun reflect off the rippling water of the lake. It was Friday, and she was glad for the coming weekend.

She went to the closet and reached for a light grey suit and a red silk blouse. The suit jacket's long sleeves would hide the bruises on her arms, which were fading to a dull and unattractive yellow. Once she was dressed, she slipped her feet into a pair of red shoes. She paused before the full-length mirror and looked long and hard at her reflection. The woman in the mirror looked calmly back, a faint smile on her lips. The grey suit set off the grey-blonde hair which she wore loose on her shoulders, the ends curling slightly. She decided she would look more poised if her hair was in a chignon and proceeded to brush and arrange it. If there was anything she was going to need today, it was poise.

With one last reassuring glance in the mirror, she went into the kitchen for a cup of coffee. This morning there wasn't any room for food in her stomach since it seemed to be full of fluttering butterflies.

Once she was behind her desk, she made a conscientious effort to treat the day like any other day but every time Louise buzzed her or the phone rang, her heart went into her throat.

At eleven, Elliott entered her office and told her the main part of the pencil collection was being installed and that he had met the Honorable J. P. Ravenel himself.

Elliott sprawled his long body into the chair by her desk and said, "You know, he made me feel like a schoolboy standing in front of the principal awaiting a decision whether I would be flogged or rewarded with a lollipop."

Dana smiled. She couldn't imagine Elliott

being intimidated by anyone but she knew what he meant. “How long is he going to be at the museum?”

“Not much longer. He was brought up in the elevator because he is in a wheelchair and looks tired but seemed satisfied with the display. Mr. Josef was all puffed up with pride after J.P. got through with his compliments.”

“So we have another successful exhibit,” said Dana drily.

Elliott grinned. “It looks that way. Can’t you just see the kids coming in with their parents and seeing these valuable pencils, then going on about how they won’t be able to do any homework with a pencil because it is valuable?”

Dana chuckled. “At least we have helped give the children a new excuse for not doing their homework. We have contributed something to society.”

Elliott got to his feet. “The school teachers may not agree with you. Besides, old Josef won’t be welcoming many kids in the museum. You know how fussy he is.” He fiddled with the pen set on her desk, arranging it to his satisfaction, oddly hesitant as his attention remained on the pen set. “I take it you aren’t too anxious to rush to the museum to renew your acquaintance with the Ravenels?”

With a grimace, Dana replied with feeling, “You are so right.”

“You know, I can’t quite place him but I think I’ve seen J.P.’s son before. He looks familiar.”

Dana forced her expression to remain unchanged. Of course Bass looked familiar to Elliott. Terry was a small replica of Bass Ravenel except for Terry’s blonde hair, which would darken as he got older.

Elliott cleared his throat and said bluntly, “I was asked by Mr. Ravenel to tell you to come to the museum. If you want me to make excuses, I will. I know you are not exactly wild about the Ravenels and it’s none of my business but if it is any help, I’m on your side.”

Biting her lip in indecision, Dana admitted, “I know I’ve been acting strangely regarding the Ravenels. I apologize for that. In a couple of weeks the collection will be gone and everything will be back to normal.”

“Will you be coming to the museum?” he prodded.

She mustered up all her composure and prepared to meet her responsibility. With an odd catch in her voice, she murmured, “I feel like a bullfighter going into the arena for the first time and dreading the moment of truth. In this case, J.P. is the bull and my cape is full of holes."

Elliott patted her firmly on her back, nearly toppling her and chuckled, "You'll manage." As they left the office, he added, "I'll go along for moral support."

Dana knew that he was also extremely curious, but she did feel more confident with him at her side.

They walked past the rare book store and went into the museum. It took their eyes a moment to adjust to the change from the bright sunny walkway to the more subdued light of the museum as they headed for the room where the pencil collection was on display. Dana's heels tapped loudly on the marble tile floor and sounded sacrilegious in the toned-down atmosphere.

Ahead of them an assemblage of people gathered around a white-haired figure in a wheelchair: J. P. Ravenel. Bass was standing near a partition a distance away but Mr. Josef and several assistants plus a woman in a nurse's uniform stood as if in royal attendance to the monarch.

To her surprise, as they approached the group Elliott walked up to Bass and said lightly, "It took a bit of doing to get her away from her desk, Mr. Ravenel, but she can spare you a few minutes." He smiled charmingly, "She is a very dedicated employee."

Bass looked down at her with a slow smile that did funny things to her insides. "How many minutes can I have?"

She was so surprised that it was Bass and not J.P. that had asked for her that she answered without thinking, "It depends on what you plan on doing with them."

She felt her cheeks get hot with color as she realized she had given him a flirtatious answer. She had the horrible feeling her face was the color of her red shirt. The only response from Bass was a broader smile.

As she heard the motor of a wheelchair, Dana turned toward the sound and knew this was confrontation time. That he had been ill was quite apparent as she noted the changes in his features since she had last seen him. His hair was almost completely white instead of the dark brown she remembered. His face was more lined and his eyes weren't as piercing as before. She couldn't tell by his expression whether or not he recognized her.

Elliott introduced Dana. "Mr. Ravenel, this charming lady is my assistant, Miss Donatus. She is responsible for the arrangements of your exhibit."

The older man's pallor was more pronounced as he repeated "Donatus?" His eyes focused intently on her face. "Dana Donatus?"

She nodded and stood still as he studied her thoroughly. He stared at her for several uncomfortable moments, his color gradually returning. Dana could feel Bass watching them closely.

Finally J.P. said tautly, "Well, Dana! To say I'm surprised to see you would be an understatement."

Bass came closer, stopping near his father's chair in a protective attitude waiting to hear her reply. She felt a twinge of irritation. What did he expect her to do? Start clawing his father's face? She would have preferred no audience at this first meeting with her old enemy but Bass was not going to allow that.

In a tight controlled voice, Dana said, "So you remember me. I didn't think you would. It's been a long time."

With a grim smile, J.P. replied, "It's not something one forgets when a young girl tries to —" As if suddenly remembering the others around them, he changed what he was going to say although Dana knew what he was referring to. "I must admit I didn't recognize you but then you were very young when I last saw you." He turned his head toward his son. "Have you met Miss Donatus, Bass?"

"Yes. When we made the arrangements for the collection."

J.P. gave Dana an enigmatic glance. "Oh, yes. The pencil collection. So I have you to thank for the artistic layout of the display?"

"No," Dana answered bluntly. "I only handled the paperwork. Mr. Josef is in charge of the museum displays. You apparently find the exhibit satisfactory?"

"Very much so."

Watching his face for a reaction, she stated, "I would like to see the Commandment pencils. I understand you brought them with you today."

"That is correct."

She continued, "I heard there are ten pencils in the collection now."

His hands tightened on the armrests of the wheelchair and his skin paled even more. Bass noticed both and moved fractionally so he was between his father and Dana as if he were a shield of protection. "That's enough." His dark eyes held flints of steel as he looked long and hard at Dana before turning to his father. "I think you should rest now. You have done enough this morning."

Aware of the tension between the Ravenels and Dana, Elliott broke in tactfully, "I would like to take everyone to lunch if Mr. Ravenel feels up to it." He included Mr. Josef as he glanced around at the group.

Dana looked at Bass and saw his eyes narrow angrily as he returned her gaze. For God's sake, what kind of threat did he think she represented to his father? The collection was on display for people to look at and admire and she was curious to see the pencil she knew she had broken. How could that represent a threat to J.P.? A sudden thought came into her mind. Possibly Bass knew the pencil was a fake and was covering up for his father.

"Don't include me, Elliott. I really must get back to work."

Dana wasn't about to spend any more time with the Ravenels than was absolutely necessary. If Bass was going to listen and analyze every word she said, she would be tongue-tied and on the defensive all through lunch.

Elliott blurted out in surprise, "Really?" He looked at her oddly, then understood what she was trying to say. "Of course, Dana. I'll see you later at the office."

With a nod of agreement, she said, "Excuse me," and started to turn away from them when firm fingers closed around her slim wrist and she was pulled to Bass's side. He spoke to Elliott, "Miss Donatus needs to eat lunch sometime. She might as well have it now. With us." He then turned to his father. "How about some lunch, J.P.? Do you feel up to it?"

His words held a double meaning to Dana but she remained rigidly silent.

Because she couldn't think of a way to get out of it without causing a scene, Dana went to lunch with the group. In the conference room of the Brass Rail Restaurant, place to accommodate the wheelchair was made at the table, and Dana was seated across from J.P. and next to Bass. She groaned inwardly.

The conversation was general as the waiter took their orders. When he left, J.P. asked Elliott about operating such a large business.

Dana sat as if frozen solid, letting the talk drift around her, unaware her hands were tightly clenched together in her lap until a warm touch gently pried them apart. Startled, she jerked her head around to look at Bass but he was looking at Elliott who was talking to J.P. A corner of his mouth curved slightly as if he were aware she was looking at him. He withdrew his hand and reached into his pocket for a pack of cigarettes, offering one to her.

Hating herself for her weakness, Dana nodded and began to reach for a cigarette but he put one to his mouth and used his lighter to light it. His hand came up to the cigarette and with two fingers he removed it, turned it around, and placed it between her parted lips.

Dana's fingers came up to the cigarette as she looked at him, her eyes wary and vulnerable. The intimate gesture threw her off balance. She could feel the warmth of his mouth on the end of the cigarette and quickly looked away as a rush of sensual excitement flowed through her.

After the meal Dana was starting to relax when J.P. suddenly turned to her and asked, "How is your mother, Dana?"

She flinched in surprise at the sudden question. "I . . . don't know."

"I beg your pardon?" J.P. asked with a puzzled frown.

"I haven't seen or heard from her in years so I don't know how she is," she said in a tight voice.

After a long moment, J.P. murmured thoughtfully, "I see. It's to be expected, I suppose."

Thankfully Elliott was talking to Mr. Josef and not listening to their exchange — but Bass was. He asked, "Why was it expected?"

She looked at him but he was addressing the question to his father who replied with a slight shrug of his shoulders, "These things happen. Sometimes for the best," which was no answer at all and Bass knew it.

He gave her a probing glance, his eyes searching hers thoroughly, but thankfully he didn't press the issue. She swallowed nervously, knowing he would bring it up at another time.

J.P. set his water glass down and asked, "What ever happened to that art career you were going to have? If I remember correctly, you were going to art school after you graduated from high school."

Hating this polite inquisition, Dana drew on her cigarette, unaware that her hand shook as she held the cigarette to her mouth. In a muffled voice, she answered vaguely, "I changed my mind. I decided I wasn't very good anyway."

She was aware that Bass had stiffened beside her. His voice drifted toward her. "So you haven't had any formal art training at all?"

Knowing he had seen the painting of Terry and had thought it good enough to buy, she glared at him, daring him to contradict her. "It would have been a waste of time. It's difficult to make a living by selling paintings unless the artist does exceptional work . . . and I needed to have a regular income to count on."

J.P. was plainly puzzled. "Your father was

a wealthy man, Dana. I wouldn't think money would be a problem."

Tired of the questions, Dana snapped, "For fear of being rude, Mr. Ravenel, it's my business what I do with my life."

Everyone's attention turned to Elliott as he pushed his chair back. Much to Dana's relief, he made suitable comments about the pleasant time spent with them all and brought the lunch to an end.

It was relatively easy to get away from the Ravenels after that. Bass helped his father out of the restaurant and Dana hurried back to her office. During the rest of the afternoon, she half-expected Bass to come to her office to resume his cross-examination but he never did.

Just before she was due to leave her office at five, the phone rang and she was greeted by Bass's deep voice. "Dana, I want to see you tonight. I'd like to take you out to dinner."

Shock made her voice waver. "I have other plans."

"Then how about lunch tomorrow?" he went on persistently.

"I'm busy."

She could almost feel his anger and impatience over the phone. "Dana, we have to talk. You name the time and place then."

Her fingers tightened on the phone until her knuckles were white. "We have nothing to talk about, Mr. Ravenel. I've been on the witness stand enough the last couple of times we've met. I don't feel like answering any more questions about my personal life, which is none of your business. For once, take no for an answer."

His voice held a hint of a threat. "Not this time, Dana. We are going to talk and I'll make sure that you don't have a choice."

The dial tone was loud in her ear as she finally realized he had hung up on her. She rested her head in her hands with her elbows on the desk. Damn him! Why wouldn't he leave her alone?

That evening, Dana took her brother to a movie.

Terry enjoyed the Walt Disney film — what he saw of it between trips to the snack bar. But as she expected, it was impossible to block Bass Ravenel and his father from her mind.

After the movie was over they got into her car and started for home. Their route took them past the Village, and Terry reminded Dana of the oar Colby had carved for him to use with the canoe they were building. Since they wanted to launch the canoe this weekend, Terry asked his sister to stop at her office and pick up the paddle. She had meant to bring it home from work, but with all that had happened during the day she had completely forgotten about it.

After parking the car at the curb, they started up the stairs to the third floor, their rubber-soled shoes making very little sound on the wooden walkway.

Dana was about to put her key into the outside door to her office when she saw a small beam of light flash in the museum. At first she thought it was the security guard or a reflection of light from the street lamp, but then she noticed the front door of the museum was open several inches. The guards had specific instructions about the front door never being opened after closing, and since they were extremely reliable, she knew something was wrong.

Dana quietly opened the office door and pushed Terry inside. She sat him down at Louise's desk and told him not to turn the light on. The glow from the street lamp outside her window enabled them to see their way around the office furniture without bumping into anything.

Dana knew she had to act quickly. She instructed Terry to call Elliott at home and tell him to come to the museum right away.

She wrote down Elliott's number for him, making sure he could see the telephone well enough to be able to dial accurately. Then she firmly told him to go to the car after he had finished making the call and that under no circumstances was he to leave it until she got there.

She knew there was a chance that she was over-reacting but the events of the last couple of days had taken a toll on her nerves and she was in no mood for things to go wrong.

Dana left Terry sitting at the desk feeling very important and grown-up about accomplishing this task.

She walked as quietly as she could toward the museum door, stepping carefully on the wooden walkway. As she neared the door she again saw a flicker of light around one of the partitions. She eased the door open, and to her dismay, it gave a hint of a squeak as she carefully pushed it open. She entered the museum and edged her way along the side of the wall praying she wouldn't knock over any of Mr. Josef's priceless sculptures standing on their pedestals. There was no sign of the light now but she headed in the direction she had last seen it.

As she was slowly making her way toward the middle of the partition where she had seen the light, she heard muffled footsteps drawing near and then felt a blinding pain on the side of her head as something struck her. Complete darkness enveloped her as she fell to the floor.

Dana had no idea how long she had been unconscious but it must have been some time because when she finally opened her eyes, she was lying on the couch in Elliott's office. Elliott, several policemen, and Bass Ravenel were standing around her.

Elliott was insisting a doctor be called for her, but she forced herself to say she was all right. Every word she spoke sent spears of pain through her head. A cold, wet wash-cloth had been placed on the side of her forehead where she had been hit and she started to remove it but Elliott snatched it away and went into the washroom where she heard water running briefly. When he came back and the cold cloth was placed on her bruised forehead, Dana was beginning to feel the office might stop spinning soon.

Elliott sat down in a chair pulled up near the couch and asked seriously, "Do you feel like talking yet?"

"I suppose so." She pulled herself up further so that she was half-sitting against the end of the couch. She felt too defenseless lying down. "What happened?"

"We were hoping you could tell us," stated Elliott, with a hint of humor and relief that she was going to be okay.

Dana quickly glanced in Bass's direction but dropped her eyes when she encountered his fierce glare. Briefly she began to outline why she had gone to the museum. Because of Bass's presence she was guarded, her explanation stilted and somewhat disjointed in her attempt to leave out any mention of Terry.

Apparently satisfied with her story, Elliott proceeded to tell her what they had found in the museum. "Your entry into the museum evidently scared off whoever had been there. The security guard was found asleep on the floor in the rear of the museum, and it looks like some kind of sleeping drug had been put into his thermos of coffee. The police have taken him to the hospital and we will talk to him when he comes around."

One of the policemen, a tall husky man dressed in a uniform badly in need of a good pressing, offered, "Nothing was taken, damaged, or even touched that we could tell but we will have a crew of experts out tomorrow to go over the place for fingerprints if it's requested." He looked at Elliott in expectation since the request would have to come from him.

Elliott ignored him for a moment. "What bothers me is the guard being drugged. To me that implies someone had planned this entry carefully. He wanted in and out without any fuss. He had a specific reason for being there and I'll be damned if I can figure out what it would be." Then he acknowledged the policeman's earlier statement. "Aside from Dana getting hurt, I can't see that anything has been damaged or taken. I can't imagine any good would come of a battery of men going through the museum with a fine tooth comb . . . or whatever it is you do. If this man is professional enough to drug a guard, he won't be the type to leave any fingerprints."

The policeman persisted, "Any new items in the museum he might have been interested in that you can think of at the moment?"

Elliott answered him impatiently, "We can check with Mr. Josef in the morning." His concern was for Dana at the moment and all this questioning was becoming irritating.

The voices buzzed around her as they continued to discuss the break-in but Dana couldn't concentrate on what they were saying. She sat up slowly, every move creating a painful stab in her head. She interrupted, "I'd like to go home, Elliott. I didn't see anybody, just heard footsteps and saw a light so I can't be of any help to you."

Elliott turned back to her and knelt down by her. "I think you had better come home with me and let Marion nurse that head of yours."

"No. I'd rather go home, Elliott. Edith will be there. I'll be fine."

Bass spoke behind Elliott. "I'll drive her home."

Remembering Terry outside in her car, she practically shouted "NO!" which surprised everyone and sent a lightning flash of pain through her head.

Elliott's voice held a touch of reproach. "You can thank Mr. Ravenel for finding you in the museum. He was walking by the Village and saw you up on the walkway on your way to the museum. Without his prompt action, you could still be there. For all we know, he could have scared the intruder away before you were hurt worse."

Before she could say anything, she heard a familiar boyish voice from the doorway. "Dana, why are the policemen here?"

Terry then saw her holding the cloth to her head and rushed across the room to sit beside her, his youthful face full of anxiety. "Dana, are you hurt?"

She smiled shakily to reassure him as she

looked down at him. Her throat was too choked with apprehension to say anything.

The silence in the room became noticeable to her then. She lifted her head and saw Elliott looking first at Terry then at Bass and back again to Terry. The confusion in his face was changing to comprehension as he realized why he had felt he had seen Bass before.

Her troubled gaze went to Bass to see his reaction. He was staring at the boy. Slowly, as if in a daze, he took the few steps between him and Terry and bent down to put his hand under Terry's chin to tilt the boy's face up toward his searching eyes. He stared long and hard at Terry before he removed his hand. She cringed under the look of fury he threw in her direction.

Terry frowned at this unorthodox treatment by the hands of this stranger and looked at his sister with a questioning expression and then back at the man.

Elliott tactfully escorted the two policemen out into the exterior office during Bass's examination of the boy and the three of them were left alone.

Bass said harshly, "Would you like to explain this?"

She knew he meant Terry and she was in no mood to talk to Bass right now. Also she didn't want anything said in front of Terry so she started to stand up. She heard a groan and realized it was coming from her. Bass grabbed one of her arms and Terry held the other as she attempted to get to her feet. The room spun for a few moments but it gradually became easier to stand.

In a rather shaky voice, she instructed Terry, "Get my purse and then we'll go home."

"Where is it?"

"I think I left it on Louise's desk. Go see."

He looked at his sister. "Dana, I tried to call Elliott but the line was busy. I kept trying, but finally I saw this man go toward the museum so I went to the car like you said. You were gone so long I thought I better see where you were."

"It's all right, Terry. Please go get my purse now."

After he left, she attempted a few steps and leaned on the desk waiting for Terry's return and for an explosion from Bass, who stood self-contained and silent beside her. She would have liked to know what he was thinking but couldn't tell anything from his expressionless face.

In a minute or two, Terry came back into the room and handed her the purse, the paddle in his other hand.

Bass looked at the boy. "Let's get you home." His arm went around Dana's waist to give her support and he told Terry to go ahead of them to the open doors. He started to walk and guide her but she balked.

"I can drive. There is no need for you to come."

"Don't be a bigger fool than you have been already," he grated in a low voice.

They walked out of Elliott's office and into the reception area where Elliott stood alone. He had put off the police until tomorrow.

Bass dismissed him. "I'm taking Dana and . . . the boy home. I'll contact you in the morning in case the police want me to make a statement."

Elliott was not to be dismissed so easily. "Dana, would you like me to take you home? You can settle . . . this when you are stronger." He indicated Terry and Bass in his glance before looking back at her.

She was at the point of agreeing with his suggestion but the arm around her tightened, silencing her.

"They are coming with me," Bass said in a voice that sent chills down Dana's spine. Looking at the boy standing by the door, he added grimly, "This is more my business than yours, Pollock, and you know it."

Elliott conceded the point and said gently, "If you need us, Dana, all you have to do is call."

Dana nodded numbly and let herself be led through the office. The three of them progressed slowly toward Bass's car parked across the street at the motel. The fresh air was reviving Dana somewhat and she was feeling a little stronger. "What about my car?"

"I'll see that it is returned to you in the morning."

When they reached his car, Bass took the paddle from Terry and put it in the back seat as if it was a perfectly natural thing for them to take along. He told Terry to get into the back seat and then helped Dana into the passenger's seat in the front.

About ten minutes later Bass drove into the driveway of the cottage and shut off the headlights and the engine. He came around to Dana's side to help her out, still not saying a word.

Before they reached the door, it was opened by a startled Edith who gasped when she saw Bass, recognizing him immediately. Then she noticed Dana was holding her forehead and helped her friend into the house. Dana was led to the plump sofa in the living room where she sat down carefully.

"What happened to you?" Edith whispered.

Before she could answer, Bass told Terry to get the paddle out of the car and bring it into the cottage. He then asked Edith for a couple of aspirins, following her as she went to get them. Dana was left alone for a few minutes but she could hear the murmur of voices from the kitchen area.

He came back alone with a glass of water and two tablets, handing them to her. She swallowed the tablets and set the glass down on the table in front of the sofa. The pain in her head was nothing compared to the apprehension she felt knowing Bass wasn't about to leave until he had an explanation about Terry.

Terry came in with the paddle and took it into his room. When he came back, he approached the sofa.

"Do you have a headache?" he asked when he saw her holding her head as she rested her elbow on the arm of the sofa.

"A little." She let Terry know that it was time for bed "You will want to get plenty of rest so you can get up early to launch the canoe, won't you?"

He nodded and said a polite goodnight to Bass before he gave Dana a light kiss on the cheek. With one last glance in their direction, he shut the door to his room.

Dana heard a few noises in the kitchen and then heard Edith's door close. Edith wouldn't be coming back to the living room anymore tonight. What had Bass said to her in the kitchen?

Bass stood by the fireplace looking down at the dead ashes, an unreadable expression on his hard features. He took out a cigarette and lit it with shaking hands, showing he was more affected by what he had discovered than she thought. He was keeping a tight control on his feelings and she was at a loss as to what those feelings were. Anger? Shock, of course. Everything that came to her mind to say seemed ridiculous so she remained silent, dreading what was to come.

# Chapter Six

After several long minutes of uncomfortable silence, Bass asked, "Is there anything to drink?"

"Top shelf of the cabinet," she answered, indicating its location with a move of her hand.

He took out a bottle of brandy and poured a shot for each of them. Sitting in a chair several feet away from her, he stared into the glass and slowly swirled the brandy around.

His expression was grim and he stated sardonically, "Now I know why you hate my father."

Unsure of his deductions concerning Terry, she asked hesitantly, "What do you mean?"

"Oh, come on, Dana," he said savagely, his eyes blazing as he looked at her. "It's obvious. I know that boy isn't mine so he must be my father's." He stood up and moved back to the fireplace. He stood tall and threatening as he looked down at her. "If you were telling the truth about only seeing my father once, you must have been an easy conquest to have slept with him the first time you were with him."

The color drained from her already pale face. He thought Terry was her child! She almost choked on the tight feeling in her chest. It felt like she had been hit a harder blow than the one on her head.

"I suppose he got what he wanted from you and then dumped you." Bass swallowed the remaining brandy in one gulp. "Yes, that would make you hate him, especially since you were left with a souvenir of the brief affair. You expected more than a one-night stand and became bitter when he was satisfied with just that."

Dana felt suddenly light-headed and reached for the brandy glass she had set down on the table, but her hand was shaking so much the amber liquid spilled onto the floor so she put the drink back down.

His voice continued bitterly. "Not that I can blame my father for what he did. If you looked anything like you do now, he can be excused for taking what you offered. You are an attractive woman, Miss Donatus. That cool unapproachable look is a challenge to any male. I've been foolish enough to be attracted to you. It's just as well I found out about my father's child before I made a bigger idiot of myself. I've never cared for leftovers." He paused as his eyes drilled into hers relentlessly. "And to think I felt sorry for you at lunch today."

Dana took a deep, shaky breath and whispered hoarsely, "Stop it. Don't say anymore." She cleared her throat and in a louder voice protested, "You've made your point."

Her reaction wasn't what he had expected. He saw her white face and shaking hands for the first time, even though he had been looking at her during his raging tirade. She looked frail and defenseless and hurt. He quickly looked away so he didn't have to witness her pain and went to refill his glass. When he turned back to her, she hadn't moved. She was sitting in a numbed silence, unable to defend herself as her head spun with his accusations.

Cursing under his breath, he held his glass to her lips forcing her to drink some of the brandy. She coughed as the liquid burned down her tight throat and she reached up to push his hand away.

He moved away from her. His next words were hard and gritty. "So what happens now? Am I supposed to forget I've seen the boy? Or do I tell my father of his new responsibility?"

Her voice was husky. "He is my responsibility."

"Doesn't my father have any rights to the boy at all?"

" 'The boy' has a name. It's Terry."

"All right," he growled. "My father has a right to know about Terry."

Dana was still shaken but the brandy had restored her enough that she discovered she still had some fight left in her.

"He's taken everything else from me. He is not taking Terry." She met his gaze, her eyes bright with shock, her voice brittle with agonizing memories. "Yesterday you were worried about your father's health when you called to tell me he would be at the Village. Do you think he could stand the shock of discovering he had a seven-year-old child?"

She saw his eyes narrow as he considered her words. Her voice was full of acid as she added, "He would also get one hell of a shock if you told him I was the boy's mother."

It was Bass's turn to be shocked. His head jerked toward her, his tall body rigid with surprise. "I think you had better explain that remark."

The pounding in her head was gradually lessening as she stood up unsteadily and walked toward the window. The view usually calmed her and made her feel peaceful, but it didn't have that effect tonight. She glanced at Terry's door to make sure it was closed. She clasped her arms in front of her as she sighed heavily. She would have to tell him the truth.

With her back to him, she began her story. "Your father was having an affair with my mother and my father and I came home one Sunday and . . . found them . . . together in my parent's bedroom . . . in bed." She closed her eyes for a moment. She wasn't doing this very well.

She took a steadying breath and went on, "We were supposed to be gone all day but our plans were cancelled because of the weather."

Bass came closer to hear her words, but she was unaware he had moved.

"When he saw them together . . . in his bed, my father grabbed his chest and collapsed. He was a lot older than my mother and had a slight heart condition which was my mother's excuse later for . . . being with J.P. She didn't even go to the hospital with my father. She stayed at the house with J.P. and I went instead. My father had tubes in his arms and wires were on his chest attached to some machine when they let me in to see him. He was on oxygen and —" Her voice cracked but she continued, unable to stop now. The words tumbled out, not in a clear concise pattern, just one memory after the other.

"He smiled at me and said he felt like a stereo. When he saw my face, he told me to cheer up, that only the good die young so he would be around for awhile but I could tell he didn't really believe it. He . . . held my hand and murmured he didn't mind. I was never sure if he meant he didn't mind about my mother having an affair or he didn't mind dying."

She shivered spasmodically, remembering how small and vulnerable the big man had looked surrounded by all the hospital machines and the nurses and doctors. "Several hours later, he was dead."

Slowly, she turned around, her eyes brilliant with unshed tears. "His death is the reason I hate your father."

It was silent in the room for several minutes. Her head was beginning to ache worse, so she went back to the couch and tucked her legs under her. She stared straight ahead, unable to stop the flood of words now that she had begun.

"I returned to the house about eight o'clock that night and J.P. was still there. I think I went a little crazy when I saw him still in my father's house. My father was dead because of the shock of seeing his wife with another man, and J.P. didn't even have the decency to leave."

Bass said quietly, "You don't have to say any more, Dana."

She laughed harshly. "Why? Do you still prefer your version? I'm sorry to disappoint you." Her voice hardened with hate. "I never slept with your father. The very thought nauseates me. That's why I'm telling you what really happened."

She failed to notice the pallor under his tan as he looked down at her. "I meant I can see that it hurts to talk about it."

With fairly steady fingers, she managed a reviving sip of brandy. "Then don't look at me if it bothers you, because I'm not finished. There is Terry yet to be explained." Without looking at him, she asked, "Do you have a cigarette?"

When she had a cigarette in her fingers, she watched the smoke spiral up into the air after he had lit it for her. "After that night, I never saw your father again. Did I mention that I tried to kill him?"

She heard his quick intake of breath and smiled ruefully at him. "As you know, he is still very much alive, so you can see I wasn't very successful." She added softly, "My heart was very much in it at the time."

Bass sat down in the chair. "I can understand why you are so bitter but why place all the blame on my father? Your mother was just as guilty as he was."

"Oh, yes, how careless of me to exclude my mother," replied Dana in a resigned tone as if she had gone halfway across a difficult bridge and knew she had to continue in order to reach the other side. "We existed in the same house for several months after that. She may have seen J.P. during that time but I doubt it. Anyway when she discovered she was pregnant, she asked me what she should do." She laughed bitterly, "I was sixteen and she was forty and yet she asked me what she should do."

She stubbed out the cigarette in the ashtray and continued, "She wanted to get an abortion but I talked her out of it. One life had been lost. It didn't seem right to purposely take another life as well. Besides she wasn't sure whose child it was . . . my father's or . . . your father's." She sighed, "To make a long story short, I had been left all of my father's property and money so I went to the trustees who were handling everything until I became of age and made arrangements to sell the house and we moved to Des Moines. When Terry was born, my mother wanted to give him up for adoption but I . . . I couldn't let her do that. I signed over my father's money to her on the condition she agree to let me keep Terry. She didn't understand why I wanted to take on the burden of a child that wasn't even mine but if the child was my father's, the baby would be a living part of him. No matter whose child he was, Terry was still part of the family. As you saw earlier, 'the boy' is definitely not my father's child."

"And your mother?"

"My mother left shortly after she was in possession of the money. Then Edith, Terry, and I moved to Clear Lake. When I became of age, I adopted Terry legally." She met his eyes. "I'm his guardian and I am responsible for him."

Suddenly she felt drained and exhausted as the words and emotions of the past hour took their toll. Her head still ached, and she desperately wanted to go to bed and close her eyes to shut everything out in blessed, healing sleep. She also had to admit she felt a strange sense of relief, as if a nagging toothache had finally stopped hurting.

She felt the cushion give beneath her as Bass sat down beside her, and she flinched when she turned to see him sitting close to her.

"For God's sake, Dana. Don't look at me

like that. I'm not going to hurt you," he said half-angrily.

"You rather enjoyed it earlier."

"I know words aren't enough to make up for the rotten things I said to you, but I was wrong and I'm sorry." He watched her hand come up to her forehead. "Is your head bothering you?"

"A little," she answered wearily.

His hard hands were surprisingly gentle as he turned her until her back was to him and began to massage the cords in her neck, soothing the tired tense muscles.

When he felt her stiffen at his touch, he muttered, "Relax. You're too tense."

"I don't know what to expect from you."

There was a humorous inflection in his voice. "Sometimes I don't either. My own reactions surprise me where you are concerned. At least now I know why you wouldn't sell me the painting of Terry. You were afraid I would see the resemblance, weren't you?"

She nodded with her eyes closed, his hands working magic along her neck and back as his probing fingers soothed the ache in her head. "Your reactions won't be tested much longer."

"What's that suppose to mean?"

"You will be going back to Ravenel Farms."

He replied absently, “Maybe.”

She opened her eyes and turned around to face him. “Are you staying for the opening on Monday?”

“I planned on it.”

“J.P. will be there too?”

“Yes.” His hands fell away from her, but he continued to watch her intently with his penetrating dark eyes.

“And after that?”

“J.P. goes back to Ravenel Farms.”

A puzzled frown appeared between her eyes. “Aren’t you going with him?” she asked, dreading to hear his answer.

His voice was casual. “I was going to . . . until tonight.”

She drew away and stood up. She took several steps away and stopped, aware that Bass had gotten to his feet and was standing near her.

With amazing coolness, he spoke behind her. “We have to talk about Terry sometime, Dana. You’ve had enough tonight so I won’t press it now but —”

“I never should have told you.”

“I’m glad you did. You have kept it to yourself too long as it is.”

“Edith knows about Terry.”

“Edith?”

“The woman who met us at the door. She

was our housekeeper and was there when . . . everything went wrong," she finished lamely.

"But I know about him now and he is related just as closely to me as he is to you. He is my half brother."

Holding her breath, she murmured, "So?"

Impatiently, he snapped, "Not tonight, Dana. You look like a fragile flower stem, due to break any minute. You need some rest before we discuss this any further."

He saw the fear in her eyes and it made him angry. "I won't take Terry away from you, Dana, if that's what is worrying you, but he is a Ravenel."

She repeated belligerently, "So?"

"Don't bait me, Dana. I might forget you have been injured. I just told you I'm not going to take Terry away from you. But I would like to get to know him. It isn't every day I discover I have a half brother I never knew existed."

Dana turned from him, not knowing what to say.

He challenged harshly, "You don't trust me."

Her attitude was making him angry, but she didn't know how she could change it. The fear had been with her too long. "I . . . I don't know."

"Come on, Dana. Either you do or you don't."

His hand grabbed her shoulder, twisting her around to face him. Surprised, she looked at his blazing eyes. His hand loosened its grip on her shoulder and slowly moved up to her throat where he could feel the pulse beating fast against his fingers. Then his hand moved down as he moved his other hand to go around her waist forcing her to remain close to him. Suddenly — too suddenly — she found herself in a crushing embrace, being kissed roughly, passionately.

His eyes were dark and unreadable as he pulled away from her. "Is this what you don't trust?" he asked softly and cruelly.

"Get out of here," she choked.

"Not yet," he answered, his eyes on her mouth. Once again, his lips claimed hers, less angry now and far more sensual. Without realizing what she was doing, she moved her hands to his broad shoulders and grasped them tightly, as if they were a lifeline in this sea of passion.

She was trembling at the scent and feel of him when she heard him say her name and instinctively knew what he was asking. Using every remaining ounce of her willpower, she managed a strangled, "No."

His body stiffened, and it seemed as if he

were debating whether or not to believe her. Almost reluctantly, he let her move away from him. Dana barely escaped the power of her own feelings as they beckoned to her to turn back into his arms.

"Do you want another apology?" he asked flatly.

She was struggling with herself, trying to make some sense out of her emotions. A part of her marveled at his composure. Her insides were disintegrating and he seemed unmoved by what had happened between them.

She slowly shook her head, finding it impossible to speak aloud. She didn't want him to be sorry he had created this sweet agony that still possessed her. Somehow that would be too humiliating.

His voice drifted toward her. "This was bound to happen."

She sighed deeply, remembering the tension between them. "I suppose so."

A threat of anger was beginning to replace the overpowering fever in her blood. He seemed so unaffected by the brief passion, as if he had taken a dose of medicine and had been cured. Her pride took over and she faced him. "Now you've gotten that out of your system, you can leave."

There were several flecks of gold in his

dark eyes as he watched her, making her feel like a fly on the end of a pin. A corner of his lips lifted as his finger reached out to brush a lock of her hair away from her face. "What makes you think I've got you out of my system?"

Forcing her features to assume a cool expression, she replied, "Wishful thinking. I don't want it to happen again."

Smiling openly now, he spoke softly as his finger moved down the side of her face and across her bottom lip. "You little liar. You didn't exactly put up a fight."

The fact that he was telling the truth didn't help her composure. She went to the door and opened it. "If you don't mind, I have a splitting headache which isn't improved by your being here."

She was a little surprised when he agreed with her. "We'll leave this until you are feeling in fighting form again. Do you think you will be able to sleep?"

"Of course," she said firmly, adding pointedly, "once I'm left alone."

His lips touched hers briefly. "I hope you have better luck than I will," and abruptly went through the doorway, leaving her staring into the darkness as the red lights of his car disappeared into the night.

# Chapter Seven

The bright Saturday morning sun was tempting as it displayed its warmth through the kitchen window and onto the table where Edith, Dana, and Terry were having breakfast.

Terry was gulping down his eggs and toast, anxious to finish so he could go outside, but his sister was telling him to slow down.

"You know you have to wait after you eat before you can go into the water so you might as well take your time. The canoe will still be there after breakfast."

"But Dana, I'm not going into the water. Only into the canoe. I can't get cramps in a canoe."

"What if the canoe tips over?"

His fork hesitated on its way to Terry's mouth. Then after he thought about what she had said, he shrugged his shoulders. Grinning, he replied, "That's okay."

Edith smiled down at the tousled-haired boy. "I think you want the canoe to tip over, young man."

He just grinned in response.

Dana took a sip from her coffee cup. "When is the launching going to be?"

Terry tipped up the glass so he could get the last drop of milk out of it. "The gang is coming over around ten. Colby is supposed to come too." Just then the phone rang, and he ran into the living room to answer it.

Edith got up and started to clear off the table, and Dana pushed her chair back to help. Terry could be heard laughing in the other room.

"That boy and that canoe," sighed Edith, shaking her head.

"He has had a great time building it, and hopefully the darn thing will last long enough for him to show it off to everyone."

Edith ran the water into the sink and added some liquid soap. "Colby has done most of the hard work and the planning but Terry gave him the incentive . . . constantly." Edith grinned. "I imagine Colby will be glad the thing is finally built so he can have some peace and quiet."

Dana grimaced. "Knowing Terry, he will probably come up with another project, bigger and better. Do we have enough to feed a hungry group of boys? Paddling a canoe is going to work up a bunch of appetites."

"There should be enough. I stocked up for the weekend yesterday." Then Edith glanced strangely at Dana who was wiping the dishes beside her. "Are . . . are you going to be home today?"

Surprised at the question, Dana stopped wiping the plate in her hand. "Of course, I am. Why wouldn't I be?"

"Well, after your . . . visitor last night and —"

Edith was interrupted by a yell from the living room just before Terry came running into the kitchen.

His sister scolded him. "Terry, I have told you time and time again *not* to run in the house."

"Oh, sorry. Hey, you know what? We're going to have a bottle of champagne to launch the canoe and I have to think of a name for it. When he asked me what I was going to do today and I told him about the canoe, he said he would bring the champagne if he could have a ride in the canoe. He told me every boat should have a name. Isn't that neat! Oh, and he said he would bring some root beer. He asked me what kind of soda I liked and I told him root beer."

"Wait a minute. Slow down. What is this about a bottle of champagne? And who is bringing it? Colby?"

"No, Dana. Not Colby. Bass. The man who brought us home last night from the Village." He raced toward the door. "I gotta go tell the other kids about the champagne."

As the door slammed behind Terry, Edith and Dana looked at each other. Dana didn't know what amazed her more, Bass coming back so soon or Terry's acceptance of Bass Ravenel whom he had just met.

Edith found her voice first. "Is that wise, Dana? Are you going to let him come here?"

"It doesn't look like I have a lot to say about it."

While they finished the dishes, Dana told Edith about the break-in at the museum, also explaining how Bass had first seen Terry. The resemblance between Bass and Terry was the reason Bass had brought her home. He had demanded an explanation and she had given it to him.

"That's what worries me, Dana. There is no mistaking the likeness between Bass Ravenel and Terry. When he arrives here and Terry's friends see them together, they might notice the similarity in looks. They also might say something about it to Terry. You know how kids are. Then what will you say to the boy?"

"I . . . I didn't think of that."

"I don't mean to interfere. You know I have your welfare and Terry's in mind when I caution you about this. I don't want you to be hurt again. And there is Terry to think of too."

Dana carefully folded the tea towel before hanging it on the towel rack behind the door under the sink. As she straightened up, she glanced out of her window and noticed her car had been returned to her. The easy way out of this situation would be to pile everyone into the car and take off, but that would be only a temporary solution.

Her face reflected the turmoil inside her, and Edith put her arm around Dana's shoulders. "Dana, I know you are young and need a man to care for you and Terry but all I'm trying to say is to take it slow and make sure you are doing the right thing."

Dana's eyes were wide with surprise. "There is nothing . . . between Bass and me. Nothing has changed. I told him what happened eight years ago because he accused me of being Terry's mother." She smiled when she heard a gasp from Edith. "I imagine it was quite a shock when he discovered his father had another son."

With a dry note in her voice, Edith declared, "He seems to have recovered nicely."

Dana just looked at her with a puzzled frown.

Edith explained, "The phone call. The champagne and root beer."

"Champagne and root beer. What a combination." Then she remembered Edith's disappearance the previous night. "Why did you go to your room last night when I returned home? What did he say to you in the kitchen?"

"He told me you had been struck on the head and that he would take care of you. He didn't come right out and say he didn't want me to stick around, but it was obvious."

Dana retorted, "Well, stick around today. I may need your support."

Soon their beach began to fill up with crowds of children of various ages and sizes. Colby arrived in his loud old car and ended up in the center of a noisy bunch of excited boys. Edith and Dana exchanged good-natured grimaces.

Barbara rang up to see if Dana still planned to go painting on Sunday. Dana had forgotten all about their plans and had to tell Barbara that it wasn't possible this Sunday and for them to go on without her. Everything was in such confusion, it was hard for her to plan even a day ahead, but she didn't mention this to Barbara.

While Edith and Dana were chatting in the kitchen, a black Mercedes pulled into the driveway carefully easing into a space between the many bicycles already there. As Dana watched from the kitchen window, she saw Bass get out of the car. She supposed it was the same car that had brought her home last night but she hadn't paid any attention then. There were so many other things on her mind.

Bass was wearing faded Levi's and a denim shirt which fitted him as if they were tailor made. The sun shone on his dark hair, finding glints of light. He looked lean, rugged, and virile . . . a combination that made a now familiar flush of heat race through her bloodstream. He went to the trunk of his car and lifted out a case of sodas with several grocery sacks perched on top of the cans. As he came near the back door, he ordered in a raised voice, "Open the door, somebody!"

Edith was closest to the door and opened it for him. After he found a vacant place on the table and had set down his burden, he turned to them and said casually, "Good morning."

"Mr. Ravenel, you have made a mess out of my kitchen. What is all this stuff for anyway?" said Edith with exaggerated severity, as she swept her arm to include the things he had brought with him.

He leaned against the counter and smiled down at her. To Dana's amazement, she saw a slight blush appear on Edith's cheeks. The Ravenel charm was in full force today.

"Canoe launchings always make me hungry, so I brought a few things to eat."

When she felt his eyes on her, Dana turned to one of the sacks and began to empty its contents. She wasn't ready to face him yet. His dark eyes roamed over her slender figure, taking in her tanned legs, white shorts and blonde hair, which was held back by a tortoiseshell clasp above the neckline of her sleeveless red top.

She began on the next bag of potato chips, hot dogs, buns, and assorted snacks while Edith directed Bass to set the case of root beer in the corner out of the way. He had even brought a bag of ice, and Edith went outside with him to get a large tub to put it in so the soda could cool.

Bass returned to the kitchen, where Dana was folding the grocery sacks. His fingers were cold from the ice when he brushed back the hair on her forehead to examine the bruise.

"How's your head this morning?"

At his touch, she found it difficult to breathe normally but managed to utter, "I'm fine." As she gently removed his hand from her forehead, she said, "Your hand is cold."

His hand grasped hers and carried it down to his side. He smiled down at her. "Warm it up with yours then."

His eyes held hers for an electric moment and she thought how strange it was that such dark eyes could hold so many different colors in their depths. The spell was broken when Terry came bursting in to insist they come see the canoe. Bass retained possession of her hand as they followed Terry outside.

The day sped by with screams of laughter and excited voices drifting along the beach and across the shimmering water. The canoe was duly christened 'Tippee Canoe' as Terry broke the bottle of champagne over the bow. Terry and Colby were the first to go out in the canoe since they had done the most work on it. They were pushed into the water with a send-off from the beach that would have made a large ocean liner proud.

To the surprise of the grown-ups, the canoe held up very well and seemed to be well constructed. Everyone had to have a ride and it took a long time to get through them all since only two could go out at one time. Edith declined Terry's invitation with dignity, using the excuse she had something to do in the kitchen.

The casualty list was light with only one scraped knee and two splinters. The food supply went lower and lower as the day progressed and the cans of root beer dwindled almost as fast as the ice melted in the tub. Edith was becoming disenchanted with the sandy feet parading through the kitchen as the children found their way to the bathroom but she decided to postpone sweeping up until later.

Bass cooked the hot dogs and hamburgers over a charcoal fire while Dana and Edith piled the picnic table full of potato salad, beans, and potato chips, making sure there was a ready supply of catsup and mustard.

As the sun began to set, the groups started to break up. Tired, sunburned children dragged themselves off to their own homes. The grass lawn and sandy beach were littered with an assortment of swimming gear, empty cans, paper plates, and towels.

After picking up the last of the debris, the three grown-ups collapsed into the lounge chairs on the patio while Colby and Terry brought the well-used canoe up onto the beach. Then Colby waved in their direction and left rather noisily in his car.

Terry came toward them with a satisfied grin on his young face. "That is one damn good boat," he exclaimed with delight as be sat down at Bass's feet.

"TERRY!"

"Well, that's what Colby said."

"You are not Colby and you had better stop using that kind of language," his sister ordered sternly.

Bass's hand reached down and tousled Terry's hair as he commented lightly, "You have to admit, Dana, that *is* one damn good boat."

She saw Terry and Bass look at each other with matching conspiratory grins. "You're a big help," she retorted, trying to sound severe but not succeeding. The sight of the two of them sitting next to each other brought the whole situation back to her after she had pushed it out of her mind for an entire day.

Terry asked Bass, "Freddie said that champagne wasn't real. It was though, wasn't it?"

"Of course. You can't christen a boat without real champagne. What did you do with the broken glass?"

Thinking a minute, Terry finally answered, "It's in a bucket by the dock. Dana said to pick it all up so no one would get cut."

"You can show Freddie the broken bottle.

The label should be in good enough shape to read."

Terry started to get up to get the bucket but was stopped by his sister. "Not now, Terry. Go take a shower first. You are covered with sand from head to foot. The bucket will still be there tomorrow."

Terry turned to Bass. "Will . . . you still be here when I'm through?"

After glancing at Dana, Bass answered, "I'll still be here."

"I won't be long," replied Terry enthusiastically and skipped into the cottage.

The sun was dropping down behind the horizon, leaving them in a dusky light. Mosquitoes were beginning to make pests of themselves, and Edith became tired of swatting them away and followed Terry into the cottage.

Dana glanced at Bass and found that he was watching her with a strange expression in his dark eyes.

His voice serious, he stated quietly, "You've done a good job with him, Dana. He's quite a boy."

"I want to keep him that way. Did you have to encourage him to swear?" Avoiding his penetrating eyes, she got up to go over to a towel lying on the ground. She hoped her nervousness didn't show and pretended to take great care in folding the towel before adding it to the pile of wet towels on a lounge chair.

"You should have heard some of the language when we were out in the canoe," he said with humor. Then he saw the tight expression on her face and added, "He knows the difference between right and wrong, Dana. He just had to express his delight with the boat and a few swear words made a dramatic effect at the time."

He levered his long body out of the chair and came over to where she was standing. "Are you afraid I'm a bad influence on him?" he asked, half-serious, half-mocking.

Hesitating briefly, she answered honestly, "Not really."

His fingers went under her chin, forcing her to meet his gaze. "I have an interest in the boy too, Dana. Have you forgotten?" He softened the hard tone of his voice by tenderly caressing her jawline with his thumb.

She swallowed nervously, his nearness having an intimidating effect as he towered over her. "No, I haven't forgotten."

He was suddenly mesmerized by the sight of the tip of her pink tongue moistening her dry lips and he felt a tightening in his body. "You're a natural, you know that?" he murmured huskily.

It was there between them again. Dana couldn't put a name on it but that didn't mean it didn't exist. It made her achingly aware of her own body in a way that confused, yet tantalized her. She clenched her fists, fighting the temptation to run her hands over his muscled chest just to see how it would feel.

Bass didn't have her inhibitions and reached out to unclasp the fastener in her hair, running his long fingers through the loosened silky tresses. "I've wanted to do that all day."

Her long lashes lifted and his dark eyes fascinated her as he began to lower his head. His mouth took hers slowly, demanding a response she gave all too easily for her own peace of mind. He kissed her expertly and thoroughly while she floundered in a sea of inexperience. Then the pressure of his mouth made her forget he was a Ravenel, forget everything but the drugging reaction of his kisses.

Her slim body arched against his in an attempt to get closer to the magic between them. All too soon, he released her, a puzzled light in his eyes.

Dana was grateful for the deepening shadows. She had the unsettling feeling her face gave away more than she wished to reveal. She was slowly becoming aware of the world again, her little world of Terry and the cottage.

"Dana?"

Refusing to meet his intent gaze, she concentrated on one of the pearl snap buttons on his denim shirt. Willing her voice back to normal, she muttered, "What?"

"When was the last time you were kissed by a man?"

His blunt question rocked her off-balance. Was she really that awkward at lovemaking? Her body stiffened in resentment, her pride wounded and sore.

"I don't think that is any of your business."

It was as if he hadn't heard her. "You appear to be remarkably untouched for a woman of twenty-five." He was discovering so many things about her, but she was still an enigma in so many ways. Knowing he had hurt her feelings, he added gently, "I'm not complaining, Dana. It's rather refreshing to find a woman willing to let the man be the aggressor and not the other way around. It does wonders for a man's ego."

His hand went to her waist to bring her back in his arms but she twisted away, unaware that her resistance only made him want her more. "You and your ego can leave anytime now. I have things to do."

His soft chuckle behind her flamed her temper. Just what she needed was for him to laugh at her. He was about to say something when they heard a young voice call out from the cottage, "Bass, where are you? I want you to see something."

Bass muttered, "I'll have to talk to him about his timing."

Terry came running out of the door, letting it slam behind him. His pajamas stuck to him in several places where he hadn't dried off thoroughly from his bath. The boy was persistent about Bass coming in with him and Bass gave Dana a look that said they would continue their conversation later.

Staring after them as they went into the cottage, Dana was amazed how easily Terry had accepted Bass into the pattern of his life in such a short time. Even Edith had put aside her doubts, at least momentarily, and had accepted his presence. She put her hand to her forehead and rubbed it as if to erase her thoughts. She didn't want to think of the impact he was having on her.

She strolled down by the water and waded in the gentle waves, her mind whirling with the Ravenels . . . J.P., Bass, Terry. She stopped. She was thinking of Terry as a Ravenel.

Wanting to hit out at something, anything to relieve this turmoil, she had to settle for picking up several rocks and flinging them one by one into the water. Finding a flat stone, she made it skip across the surface of the water several times

The back door slammed and Bass called her name. She continued throwing the pebbles into the water and didn't answer him. His dark form came toward the beach, but he didn't come directly toward her. He went to the dock and stood looking across the water. Dana glanced quickly in his direction. His face was still and serious, his hair moved slightly as the wind blew past him off the lake.

Now what? Had Bass said something to Terry? Her shoulders drooped wearily. She walked away from the water and sat down in the sand with her arms across her raised knees and laid her head on her arms, wishing he would just go away and leave them alone.

Bass came over and sat down beside her. So softly she barely heard him, he murmured, "Terry showed me the model ship he's been building in his room. While I was sitting on his bed, he came over to me and put his arms around my neck and hugged me, thanking me for bringing the champagne."

Dana was speechless at the emotion in his voice. She raised her head and looked at him.

Moonlight etched the strong lines of his face against the darkness surrounding them. "Today out in the canoe with him, seeing that little face so much like the one I see every morning in the mirror was very strange. He has a sense of humor, is bright and intelligent, and has some of my characteristics even though he's never been around me until today. I thought there was very little in life that could throw me . . . until I met you and my . . . brother."

"Half brother," breathed Dana.

He faced her, his expression hard and unrelenting, "He is as much a part of me as he is you. There is no doubt my father is his father. The resemblance is too obvious." His voice hardened, "My God, Dana, how could you have kept him from us?"

She winced as if he had struck her, her face turning pale in the moonlight. She turned her head away but turned back again when his fingers came around her neck, making her look at him. With a deep sigh, he said, "Never mind now. Let's not ruin the day by digging it all up again."

She couldn't see his face clearly since he was turned away from the moonlight, but he could see the haunted look in her eyes. "Don't look like that, Dana," he groaned. "I'm only human." He let his hand fall down to his side. "I wanted to talk to you about Terry but maybe I better leave and we will talk tomorrow. All this moonlight and water is wearing away my good intentions. I promised myself I would go slowly with you and it's nearly impossible here."

Her voice was husky with suppressed emotion. "I don't even know where you're staying."

"At the motel across from the Village West. That's how I happened to be near the Village last night when you were going into the museum."

"And J.P.?"

"Dana . . ."

"We have to talk about Terry . . . and J.P. and get this mess settled once and for all."

Rather impatiently, Bass stated, "J.P. is leaving after the opening of the exhibit and will go back to the farm. There is no reason for him to stay here. Why are you so concerned about him?"

"What will happen if he finds out about Terry?" She had to know. It's what was eating away at her.

"Nothing will happen," Bass said through clenched teeth, his patience running out.

"I'll take care of everything." After a long, uncomfortable pause, Bass got to his feet and pulled her up beside him, turning her so that they faced each other. "Dana, I have a solution, a way for Terry to become a Ravenel and still remain in your care."

Alarmed at his sudden shift of mood and what he implied, she tried to draw back but his hands were unyielding. "I knew you would interfere. I just knew you couldn't just let us be. Damn, why did you ever come to Clear Lake?"

"Just listen to me before you panic. After I left you last night, the idea came to me. We —"

Her voice rising, Dana cried, "I don't want to hear it. I want things to stay the way they are."

His anger matched hers. "Do you enjoy being a martyr to a seven-year-old boy? If you plan on sacrificing yourself for the rest of your life, you're a fool. You have no life of your own this way. Unless I'm mistaken, you haven't been out with a man in a long time, much less had a man make love to you. Is that what you want? To waste the best years of your life, never knowing how it feels to lie in a man's arms or to bear a child of your own, to wither away unloved and unfulfilled?"

She put her hands over her ears. *"Stop it."*

He pulled her hands down and held her slender wrists. "Dana, I want you to marry me."

Stunned, Dana stared at him. She couldn't have heard him correctly. "What . . . did you say?" she stammered.

"I said we will get married. That way Terry will become a Ravenel and benefit from having a man around. You will be able to have someone share the responsibility financially and in every other way. You've carried the burden long enough by yourself."

"You mean . . . get married . . . to each other?"

He half-smiled, "That's the general idea."

"But . . . that's crazy."

"Why?"

She was finding it very difficult to breathe. "We hardly know each other."

A corner of his mouth twitched. "I hear that married people get to know each other . . . very well."

She still couldn't take it in. "I can't."

"Why not?"

"I . . . I couldn't. Not like this. Not —"

He interrupted sternly. "Don't be a fool, Dana. You don't have a choice."

She trembled. Oh God, why was he doing this? Acting as cold-blooded as if they were discussing a business venture. "What would be the relationship between you and me? I mean if we get married for Terry's sake?"

"We would live like normal married people," he explained patiently. "I don't think I have to spell that out. The main thing is to give Terry his birthright. He is a Ravenel. He is entitled to share the Ravenel property. He also needs a man's guidance, something you can never provide by yourself."

She put her hands against his chest, attempting to push him away. He drew her toward him, capturing her hands between their bodies so she couldn't move them. She could feel his heart thudding rapidly against her palms indicating he wasn't as unaffected by her nearness as he appeared. The scent of his after-shave blended with the male scent of his body, stimulating and confusing her. Her mind refused to think coherently when he was so close. She had to get away from him. With force strengthened by panic, Dana pushed against him with such violence, he released her to keep his balance. She whirled around and ran along the sandy beach away from him but after only a few yards, he caught up with her

The sudden strong grip on her shoulders knocked her off-balance and she fell to the sand. Bass toppled after her, pinning her down with his weight.

She struggled against him at first but eventually lay still, exhausted mentally, emotionally, and physically.

His breath was warm against her face. "Dana, don't fight me in this. You are going to marry me. Accept it."

She choked, "You can't force me to marry you."

Bass was sitting beside Dana now, leaning over her as he pinned her arms at her sides. "I can, you know."

Her eyes were wide and frightened. "How?"

"I can tell Terry that he is my child, that you have kept him from me all these years. He likes me, Dana. I don't think he will be too disappointed to think of me as his father."

Dana closed her eyes as a sickening sensation weakened her. She felt trapped and miserable. He was right. Terry would approve of him as a father. Gradually she opened her eyes. In a strained voice, she asked, "Isn't that a bit drastic? We can come to an agreement of some kind where you can visit Terry or —"

"There is another reason." He heard her sudden intake of air as he brushed her cheek with the back of his hand. "I want you. You are a warm, compassionate woman with a hidden fire under that cool exterior that I'm anxious to kindle into a roaring blaze. I want exclusive rights to you in exchange for taking care of you and Terry and giving him his rightful name. You've felt this chemistry between us. Don't try to deny it. Just be glad I'm willing to marry you before I sleep with you."

"You're cruel," she choked, knowing what he said was true. She had felt the tension between them since the first day they met but didn't know then what caused it. Now she did.

"I'm just being honest." He propped himself up on his elbow to look at her, resting one hand lightly on her hip. "After I talk to J.P., he will think Terry is my child. The resemblance is unmistakable. J.P. will know as soon as he sees the boy that Terry is a Ravenel. He doesn't need to know Terry is really his child. The way his health is at the moment, I doubt if he could take the shock of discovering he has another son. We'll let J.P. believe what he likes about us. The main thing is to give Terry the security of a family and the benefits of being a Ravenel."

Dana felt swamped by him and frightened by his sudden control of her life. "Do you expect me to live in the same house as J.P.? After what I told you last night?"

He reached out to gently push a strand of hair away from her face. "The farm is large enough for all of us. We will work something out if you would rather not live in the main house. Face the devil on his own ground, Dana. You may find he isn't quite the ogre you've made him out to be."

"Oh God! This is impossible," she practically screamed in frustration. "You don't know what you're asking me to do."

His jaw tightened. "I'm not asking you, Dana. I'm telling you. If I gave you a choice, you would say no. Just trust me. There are certain times when good sense must be put aside to blindly follow our instincts. I have never been more certain of anything than I am that this marriage will work."

Angrily, she snapped, "That's absurd. I don't even know you."

His deep voice became provocative, leaving her with no doubts about what he meant, "You will."

With an edge of desperation in her shaky voice, Dana said, "You have to give me some time to think about this. You can't expect me to agree to such a big step right now. There is no great hurry, is there?"

Bass heaved a deep sigh. "You may not

think so, but I do." Suddenly he got to his feet in a lithe motion for such a tall man. He reached down and pulled her up to stand beside him. Cupping her face in his warm hands, he murmured, "I'll give you some time, Dana. The end result will be the same but you deserve a little time to get used to the idea."

It was humiliating for Dana to admit disappointment that he wasn't forcing her into a decision now. But it was as if he knew her better than she knew herself. If he forced a decision now, she would blame him for it. He knew she had to adjust to the idea of marrying him and come to him of her own free will.

# Chapter Eight

Sleep refused to come after Bass left. She rolled and tossed and finally gave up even trying to get any rest. Her life had suddenly turned upside down and she had no idea how to right it again. There had to be an alternative to marrying Bass Ravenel. It *would* be good for Terry to have a father figure, but what would life with Bass do to her? He had said that the marriage would be a real one, and she knew it would destroy her to give herself to a man who didn't love her.

Going over and over it didn't help, so she dressed and went outside to bring in the soiled towels. Then she took the watering can and went around to all of the various houseplants, hoping that the simple, methodical activity would make her feel halfway normal again.

By the time she had finished practically drowning every bit of greenery in the cottage, she heard Edith moving around in the kitchen. Approaching her friend, Dana said, "Don't fix me any breakfast, Edith."

"You're up early. Is there anything wrong?"

She couldn't tell Edith about Bass's proposal just yet. "Not really. I just felt like getting up early."

It wouldn't accomplish anything to tell Edith she hadn't slept at all. The older woman would worry about her. Hoping for a miraculous idea that would thwart Bass's plans, she didn't plan on saying anything.

After pouring herself a cup of coffee, she went out onto the patio and sat on one of the lawn chairs. A few minutes later, Edith came to the door to tell Dana she was wanted on the phone.

When Dana picked up the receiver, she heard a deep voice say, "Good morning, Dana."

"Hello, Bass."

"I'm calling to let you know I won't be coming out to see you today as I had planned. Something came up at the farm and I have to return."

"I see," she answered, looking down at the carpet.

He continued in a stern voice, "I want Terry to come with me."

Her head jerked up. "NO!"

"Yes." His voice was determined. "He has to get used to me sometime. This is as good an opportunity as any. It will be a chance for him to see the farm before he goes there to live."

Her legs felt weak with shock, and she was feeling slightly lightheaded. "Bass, you have no right to demand this. You don't even bother to ask me if he can go."

"Take another look at your brother, Dana," he murmured quietly, his soft voice making the words frightening. "Then tell me I have no right."

She sat down heavily in the chair by the phone. A shudder went through her as another decision was completely taken out of her hands. She ran her hand distractedly through her hair. "Oh my God." Her voice cracked with helplessness.

"Come on, Dana. It's only for a couple of days and when we get back, you both can get ready to move to the farm. For good."

She said anxiously, "Can't we discuss this first?"

Firmly, he answered, "We already have."

"You command and I have to obey?"

She heard him chuckle, his good humor restored. "Love, honor, and obey."

She gasped as he repeated part of the marriage vows. In the distance she heard a male voice talking in the background. She then heard Bass answer, "I'll be there in a minute," as if he held the phone away as he talked to the person in the room. His voice was stronger and clearer when he spoke again to Dana. "Have Terry ready in about half an hour."

The voice in the background became louder and more insistent. Dana realized it was J.P.'s voice. Without realizing what she was doing, she placed the receiver back in its cradle.

She stared at the silent phone, waiting to see if it would ring again. She stood there feeling as if she was a stick floating along in a strong current, unable to control her direction as she was carried along by a powerful force.

Bass arrived sooner than she expected, but she kept herself busy getting Terry's small suitcase packed and listening to the boy's excited chatter. She watched as Bass took Terry's suitcase to the car with Terry running closely behind him. Before Terry got to the car he stopped abruptly and ran back to Dana who stood in the doorway of the cottage. She hugged the small boy close to her for a long moment and kissed him goodbye.

Standing a few feet away from them, Bass said softly, "He's only going to be gone a few days, Dana."

She released Terry slowly and walked with him to the car, opening the door and ushering Terry into the front seat. She turned toward the cottage but was stopped by Bass's hand on her arm.

"It's only for a few days," he repeated, anger in his voice and eyes.

She turned toward him. "Is it?" She pulled her arm away. "What if I called your bluff? I don't think even you would hurt a seven-year-old boy, especially when that boy is your half brother." She placed her hands on her hips and faced him defiantly. "Well, go ahead. Tell Terry you are his father and his sister has been lying to him all these years."

The muscle in his jaw flexed as his lips thinned into a straight line and his eyes turned to steel.

When he didn't say anything, Dana prodded the devil. "You can't do it, can you? You thought you could bully me into going along with your plans and I wouldn't fight back. Well, I'm fighting you, Bass Ravenel, every inch of the way. You can't take the only person who cares about me. He needs me and you aren't going to take him from me."

Silence hung in the air between them. She wished he would say something, anything.

Her courage was beginning to fail her as she met his hostile eyes. As if in slow motion, he turned his head in Terry's direction as his hand closed around her arm, hurting her and preventing her from moving away.

He said only one word. "TERRY!"

Dana's eyes went briefly to Terry, watching the boy pause in hesitation, his young face puzzled at the tone of Bass's voice.

Bass met Dana's tortured eyes, a strange smile on his compressed lips. "Come here, Terry. I have something to tell you."

Her eyes closed in pain. She had tried and failed. Now it would be her fault if he told Terry everything he had promised to tell. Her lids flew up when she felt his arm go around her shoulders as she was pulled into his side. His mouth came near her ear. "I've played more games of poker than I can count. You're way out of your league."

Out of the corner of her eye, she could see Terry coming closer and closer to them. An anguished whisper escaped her lips, "Don't tell him. Please."

Terry asked, "What did you want to tell me?"

It took all of Dana's strength to force a quivering smile on her mouth. She felt herself go limp against the strong male body next to her and felt his arm tighten in support. She choked out the words that proved he had won. "Bass was just going to tell you that I want you to be careful when you're at the farm." She took a deep breath. "Do as Mr. Ravenel tells you. You aren't used to a farm so do as he tells you. Okay?"

Terry gave her an impatient shrug, plainly not understanding what all the fuss was about. He just wanted to be going, not standing around talking. "I'll be all right. Can we go now?"

She could feel her control slipping and stiffened her spine to stand away from Bass. "Yes, you can go now. Have a good time."

She gathered her shredded pride around her and walked into the cottage, ignoring Bass when he called her name. Her bedroom was her destination and her sanctuary. Once there, she shut the door and leaned against the wall, gradually sliding down the hard surface until she was on the floor hugging her knees as if her life depended on it. She let out the breath she had been holding in an attempt to prevent herself from crying in front of Terry and Bass.

But now that she was alone, the tears wouldn't come. She felt numb with a nameless grief, feeling as if she had just lost Terry forever. In a way she had. Now that Bass insisted on his right to see Terry and get to know him, her brother would no longer depend solely on her.

Maybe that is why she felt so bad. The feeling of being needed by someone hadn't been a burden of responsibility but a reason to live. She was being pushed aside . . . and it hurt.

Her door opened quietly and strong hands closed over her upper arms to lift her to her feet.

"You're putting yourself through hell for nothing, Dana." There was a strange catch in his voice as Bass looked down at her pale face. She was going through suffering and pain but he couldn't understand why. He knew it was real and he felt oddly helpless. She looked like a hurt child and he wanted to hold her and protect her, but he knew she would reject his sympathy.

He released his hold on her and spoke quietly, "I promise Terry will be all right."

"Of course he will. He's a Ravenel," she said bitterly. Turning away, she snapped, "Go away. You've got what you wanted."

"Not yet, Dana. That will have to wait until after we're married." His lips tightened as he saw her wince and move away. This wasn't the time to talk to her about their future plans. Very softly, he added, "You are going to have to start trusting me sometime,

Dana. I am positive that what I am doing is in the best interests of all three of us." He went to the door. "I'll bring Terry back in a couple of days. We'll talk then."

She was still standing where he had left her when she heard the car engine roar to life and then fade away.

Several hours later Dana was sitting on the edge of the dock with her feet dangling in the water. The view of the lake usually acted as a cool balm on her nerves, but nothing could ease her fear that Bass might not keep his word and not return Terry to her. What could she do about it? Take him to court and have the whole miserable mess made public? She was Terry's legal guardian but the court might change that with pressure from J.P. once he discovered there was another Ravenel in existence.

Bass had said to trust him and she really didn't have any other options at this point. If he hadn't been a Ravenel, that request would have been a lot easier to comply with. Perhaps she was being unreasonable to let her prejudice for J.P. color her feelings for his son but she had hated J.P. for so long, the hatred had become a part of her. It would take time to alter her feelings . . . and Bass wasn't prepared to give her that time.

Dana looked up to see Edith coming

down the path from the cottage, a frown on the older woman's usually serene face. Dana sighed. Now what?

"Dana, J. P. Ravenel is up at the house. He says he must have a few words with you."

"Oh God!" What did he want? Dana slipped on her sandals and started toward the cottage. "Did he say what he wanted?"

"All he said was he wanted to talk to you for a few minutes."

Dana went into the living room after reassuring Edith that she could handle J.P. alone. J.P. was sitting in his wheelchair by the window overlooking the lake. She looked around the room but found they were alone. There was no sign of his nurse.

As if reading her thoughts, J.P. commented mildly, "I took a taxi and the driver kindly helped me into the house. I thought it best we have a private talk."

Dana stood in the middle of the room looking down at the man in the wheelchair who had been responsible for changing her life drastically eight years ago. "What could we possibly have to talk about, Mr. Ravenel?"

"Sit down, for heaven's sake, girl. I'll get a kink in my neck if I have to continue looking up at you throughout our conversation."

Waiting until she was seated on the couch,

J.P. stated his reason for coming to her cottage. "My son and I had a little chat this morning before he left for the farm. He tells me he is . . . involved with you."

Her voice sounded incredibly calm, which surprised her since she was terribly nervous and apprehensive. "And you mind?"

His lips curved slightly into a smile that didn't reach his eyes. "I could say I mind but I am mostly surprised considering your attitude toward me. I wouldn't think my son would be your choice of . . . well, whatever you want to call your relationship with him."

"Mr. Ravenel, please say what you came to say. I doubt if I'll agree with you but I will give you the courtesy of listening." She paused, adding, "If only for old time's sake."

There was a hint of chill in his voice. "I see the years since our last meeting have not improved your manners." He leaned forward in his chair. "I understand Bass has asked you to marry him."

"Yes, he has." She squared her shoulders and asked, "Why does that concern you? Bass is perfectly capable of making that decision on his own. The days of arranged marriages are past."

"True, true. I'm not so unrealistic to expect Bass to marry who I choose."

"Then why are you here?"

"I was curious. Yes, I suppose that is why I'm here basically. You haven't known my son very long and suddenly Bass tells me you are going to be married. You must admit that is strange, especially since I know your feelings all too clearly about the . . . association I had with your mother. Whether you wish to believe it or not, Dana, I care about my son. He is all I have now. I would like very much to have him married and have a family of his own but I do not want him to make an error in judgment." He then said in a subtly aggressive tone of voice, "Is Bass a good lover?"

She gasped audibly at his blunt question and stared at him in disbelief as he continued, "The Ravenel men have a reputation for possessing a weakness for a pretty face . . . and . . ." His voice trailed off as he looked meaningfully from Dana's neck downward. His implication was all too clear.

Dana's face reflected the disgust and anger churning inside her. How did Bass even begin to expect her to live in the same house as this man? She saw J.P. smile as he could see the effect his words made on her.

He continued, "I admit I have always

found some women better than others but I am still surprised my son has decided to legalize his . . . association with you. He has had many affairs, you know, and once I thought he might marry a girl we had known for years but . . . well, it didn't work out and it is time he settled down. A man in his thirties should start thinking of a family, but it must be someone suitable."

He was still smiling that horrible smile as he reached into his breast pocket to bring out his leather wallet. "I would like to ensure you don't contemplate marriage with my son. An affair is quite another matter and I wouldn't think of interfering with that, but marriage is not to be considered."

He extracted a large amount of bills but Dana stopped him from offering them to her. "I don't want your money, Mr. Ravenel, so put it away."

His eyes narrowed as he gazed intently at her. "Trying for something bigger perhaps? More security? You realize he is the heir to Ravenel Farms and you would like your legal share?"

"You must have known a variety of women who only wanted money from you if you expect that is all I want from Bass. Didn't anyone ever want you for yourself, J.P.?" Seeing the astonishment on his face at her sudden attack, she answered her own question. "No. I don't suppose anyone could."

His face had taken on a flush of anger and his eyes had hardened as his resentment toward her began to build. As he continued staring at her, the wallet was returned slowly to his pocket.

A harsh chuckle suddenly exploded from the elderly man. "I sincerely hope my son is sufficiently pleased with your . . . talents, my dear girl. He can't be overly fond of your conversation. A woman is always much more entertaining in a bedroom than in the drawing room."

Dana found herself choking with outrage. He made the whole thing sound cheap and dirty. She stood up and went to the phone. With a controlled but shaky hand, she dialed a number. After a short pause, she gave the person on the phone the address of her cottage and hung up.

"A taxi will be here soon, Mr. Ravenel. When it arrives you will get into it and will not come back here . . . for any reason."

J.P. sighed. "I can see I underestimated you, Dana. Perhaps I have been too hasty in judging you."

"I don't see why it is necessary for you to have to judge me at all," Dana said through tight lips. "And there is also no necessity in offering me money. Like my father, I am refusing your money. Remember he wouldn't accept money from you for the pencil collection? You had wanted it so badly, however, you seduced my mother to get it."

"My God, girl. Who told you that?"

"My mother said that is why you originally came to the house. Then things . . . got involved."

A strange expression crossed his face. If he had been any other man, Dana would have thought it was pain. He said, "How strange. I never realized that is what your mother thought. Not that it matters at this late date. What does matter is my son. I have found that everyone has their price and fortunately I have the means to acquire whatever I want. You, however, are using other means to get what you want. I just wish I knew exactly what you did want from my son."

She couldn't quite believe they were having this ridiculous conversation. "Why not ask him?"

"I have. All he says is that you are coming to live at Ravenel Farms." His voice hardened. "I will not have you there, Dana, reminding me daily of my previous involvement with your mother, digging up the past and throwing it in my face. Bass can have his meetings with you elsewhere but not in my own home. If you hope to get back at me for the past by having an affair with my son, you will not be successful. But if you marry him, you will be the one who will regret it."

Dana could easily have put his mind at rest by telling him that she didn't plan on marrying his son but some incomprehensible side of her nature stopped her. J.P. hadn't said anything about Terry and that started her wondering whether Bass had even mentioned him.

"Did Bass mention anyone else coming with me when I arrive at the farm to live?"

Misunderstanding her, he answered smoothly, "One at a time is our motto. I might add discretion as part of that motto and not blatant display of one's lovers. I realize you are presently located at a distance from our home that would make nightly visits very wearing for Bass, so have him locate you nearer if necessary . . . but not at Ravenel Farms. He will just have to get you out of his system without going to the extreme of marrying you."

A slow smile curved Dana's lips. "We'll discuss it next time we're together and let you know what we decide."

A horn honked outside and she went to the door to beckon the driver. When the driver came to the door, she asked him to help Mr. Ravenel with his wheelchair and as she opened the door for them, she said politely, "It was nice seeing you again, Mr. Ravenel. We must do this again sometime."

There was a glint of admiration in the older man's eyes as he looked up at her. "I imagine we will."

As the taxi drew away from the house, Dana sank down onto the couch, feeling drained and exhausted. She was also surprised at her own actions. She could have told J.P. that she hadn't agreed to marry Bass but she had remained silent.

Now she wondered why.

The next morning, Dana dressed quickly and drove to the Village with little conscious thought about what she was doing. After spending the better part of the night thinking about her uncertain future and her involvement with the Ravenels, she was as far away as ever from coming up with a solution to her problems.

The day seemed endless. The enthusiasm she usually had for her job had gone flat. The daily reports were a chore to fill in and the ceaseless series of complaints from shopkeepers and customers was irritating and annoying.

With an overpowering sense of relief at the end of the working day, Dana headed for her car in the parking lot. By the time she noticed Janelle Duvall waiting for her, it was too late to avoid a confrontation. Forcing a smile, Dana approached her car and Janelle.

"Hello, Janelle. Finished for the day?"

"Yes. It was a particularly tiring day, too. We received a large order of cards today plus a back-order of stationery. My assistant had to leave early to go to the dentist so it was up to me to put the stock away as well as wait on the customers."

Dana looked at the woman in front of her, trying hard to keep a straight face. It was amazing how Janelle could put so much self-importance into her voice.

"Well, you had better hurry home and put your feet up. I'm sure you are quite exhausted," said Dana with mock-sympathy, reaching into her purse for her car keys.

Janelle missed the sarcasm altogether and took Dana seriously. "I plan to, but first I wanted to ask you something."

Dana unlocked her car door and threw her purse onto the front seat, anxious to get away. "If it's about work, can't it wait until tomorrow?"

"It isn't about work. I wanted to talk to you about Bass Ravenel."

Dana's head turned sharply in Janelle's direction. "What about him?" If the wretched woman was going to warn her to stay away from Bass, she would scream. It was just what she needed on top of J.P.'s warning.

"I know you don't know him well, not as well as I do, but I was hoping he might have said where he could be reached when he is in town. I'm having a little party next Saturday evening and wanted to invite him." She smiled archly. "He always used to enjoy my parties."

"Sorry," Dana replied stiffly. "Mr. Ravenel is out of town."

Disappointment showed in the other woman's face. But she wasn't giving up that easily. "If he happens to get in touch with your office before Saturday, would you call me?"

"Better yet, I'll just have him contact you personally," replied Dana. "If I hear from him."

"I would appreciate it. Bass and I were . . . good friends at one time and sort of drifted apart." She gave Dana a woman-to-woman look. "You know how it is."

Dana responded with a nod of her head. "I know how it is." She got behind the wheel of her car. If she didn't drive away now, she would say something rude. As she started the engine, she heard Janelle say something but Dana hadn't rolled down her window, so she pretended she hadn't heard anything and drove away.

What a perfect ending to her day at work. She glanced in the rear-view mirror and saw Janelle gracefully walking to her own car. A week ago Dana might have thought the idea of matchmaking for Bass Ravenel was funny. But she wasn't laughing now. If she didn't know better, she would think she was jealous.

About nine o'clock that evening she couldn't stay in the house another minute. She felt pressed down, smothering in the enclosed walls. Edith shook her head sadly as Dana took her car keys and left the cottage.

She drove for miles and miles seeing nothing but the ribbon of road ahead. She forced her mind to stop dwelling on the present problems and concentrate on driving instead. If she didn't stop worrying about Terry and the impossible demands Bass was making on her, she felt she would go quite mad.

A short stop at a gas station and a quick cup of coffee were the only breaks she allowed herself before getting behind the wheel again.

She finally returned to the cottage well after midnight, her eyes glazed with fatigue. To her surprise Edith was waiting up for her.

Dana slipped off her jacket and threw it onto the back of the couch. "Why are you still up, Edith? It's late."

"I was worried about you. You were pretty upset when you left. Where have you been?"

"Just driving."

"Did it help?"

"Not really. But I couldn't just sit here waiting." She laughed without amusement. "I don't even know what I'm waiting for."

Edith watched her walk to the window. "Come and sit down, Dana."

Dana slowly sat down on the couch. Her face was showing signs of exhaustion and stress, her eyes dark with pain.

Without looking up, she said, "Go to bed, Edith. I promise I won't go out again."

"When will you be going to bed, Dana? You need some rest."

"I'll just sit here for awhile. I'm all right."

She sat on the couch throughout the rest of the long lonely night staring off into space. When the first light of dawn finally came through the windows, she rose from the couch and went into her bedroom to get ready for another day.

At the office she buried herself in work, not even stopping for lunch. The thought of food almost choked her anyway. Elliott came into her office late in the afternoon and stopped abruptly when he noticed Dana's pale face, the violet circles under her eyes and the weary droop of her shoulders.

"Good grief, girl. I never realized what a slavedriver I am. Is bankruptcy just around the corner?"

Dana explained lamely, "I decided to see if I could get all this paperwork done and have a clear desk for a change."

"I am impressed with the idea although I've never been able to succeed in carrying out such a noble plan." Changing the subject abruptly, he asked, "How about coming to the house tonight for dinner? Run home after work and get Terry and spend the evening with us."

"Terry's not at home."

Elliott looked momentarily startled. "Where is he?"

Leaning back in her chair, Dana said woodenly, "He went to Ravenel Farms with Bass Ravenel."

"For how long?"

"Bass said a few days." Her tone indicated she didn't entirely believe it. "They left on Sunday."

Elliott sat down in a chair near the desk and leaned on one of the arms as he studied her carefully. "You don't look too happy about it. In fact you look like hell. Do you want to talk about whatever it is that's bothering you?"

"I suppose I do owe you an explanation. I noticed how you looked at Terry and Bass the night the museum was first burglarized."

"The resemblance left little to the imagination. I also got the impression Terry was a shock to Bass Ravenel."

Her voice was harsh and bitter. "He didn't know about Terry. He still wouldn't know if it were up to me."

"Dana, as I keep saying, it is none of my business but as a man with children and your friend, I feel qualified to butt in. I would be pretty upset if someone had a child of mine and didn't tell me. My God, a man has a claim on his own child."

Dana wearily shut her eyes for a moment. She had the feeling of having had this conversation before. When she opened her eyes, she looked straight at Elliott. "Not you too, Elliott." She sighed heavily, "Terry is not my child. Nor is Bass his father. My mother was . . . she had an affair with J. P. Ravenel. J.P. doesn't know about Terry but Bass does."

Elliott let out a whistle. "The plot thickens. I think I had better do what I am always saying I'm going to do and mind my own business. This is beyond my experience." He leaned forward in the chair. "Listen, come on home tonight. You need company. It's not good for you to be alone so much. I can give Marion a call. She always has plenty of food and you know you are always welcome. No discussions about the Ravenels. I promise."

"I'm not alone. Edith is at the cottage," she protested.

He picked up the telephone and began to dial. "Tell her to come along too." He then talked to Marion and told her there would be two extra for dinner.

The evening passed quickly at the Pollock household. The active boys kept the conversation revolving around them and their antics. Elliott and Marion believed in including their children when they entertained informally, and this made for a lively social occasion.

Several times during the evening, Dana felt Marion's concerned gaze on her but Elliott had evidently warned his wife not to ask any personal questions . . . and Dana was thankful. The warmth and unspoken caring wrapped around her like a soothing blanket, which was exactly what she needed. The message came through loud and clear. She wasn't completely alone. She had good friends who cared about her.

The following day seemed easier to get through. There was enough work to keep Dana busy although she wasn't allowed to work through her lunch hour again because Marion came into the office and insisted on Dana keeping her company at a local salad bar.

That evening when she drove into her driveway, a familiar figure burst out of the door and ran toward her.

Terry had returned.

He was full of excitement and started to tell his sister about the trip to Ravenel Farms as soon as she got out of the car.

"Bass showed me some horses that he said I could ride after he shows me how and I saw barns and —"

"Hold on, Terry. Let me at least get into the house and then you can tell me all about it." She hadn't seen Bass's car in the drive. He must have dropped Terry off and then left.

As she opened the screen door, she asked Terry, "Did Bass say when he would be back?"

"He had to go back to the farm. His father had planned to arrive at the farm and Bass wanted to talk to him."

Dana went over to the couch and sat down. "So tell me about all the things you did."

"We went fishing in a little creek that runs through one of the fields. I had a couple of nibbles but I didn't catch anything. Then Bass let me drive their sit-down lawnmower for awhile and he showed me around the farm. He's got a neat laboratory in one of the buildings with bottles and all sorts of funny looking equipment. I'm not supposed to ever go in there unless he is with me because some stuff in there can be dangerous."

Glancing down at his feet, Dana pointed at his new footwear. "I see Bass took you shopping, too."

Terry's eyes shone brightly as he admired his new cowboy boots. "I got some shirts and jeans too. Bass says sneakers aren't very safe to wear on a farm."

For the next ten minutes or so, Terry described everything he had seen and done with almost every sentence beginning with "Bass said." If Bass wanted to make sure Terry would adapt to life at Ravenel Farms, he had to be pleased with Terry's obvious enthusiasm.

When Terry took a much-needed breath, Dana asked about a package lying on the table unopened. "What's this?"

"That's for you. Bass bought it. He said to give it to you. Open it."

She unwrapped the paper carefully, removing a white earthenware pot which was decorated with flowers, butterflies, and bees. It was very pretty but Dana was puzzled why he would buy her such a thing. It was heavy so she removed the seal and pried open the lid. She stuck a finger into the opening and then licked the finger. Honey! Bass had given her a pot of honey.

When she moved the wrapping paper off her lap, a small folded piece of white paper fell onto the floor. Picking it up, she read, "To sweeten your mood."

"Do you like it?" Terry asked doubtfully. "I didn't think it would be a good gift but Bass said it would be perfect for you."

Dana stared at the pot in her hand. She didn't know whether she felt pleased or furious.

All through their evening meal and until the minute he went to bed, Terry chattered excitedly about Bass and Ravenel Farms. He never mentioned going there to live, so Dana assumed that Bass had not yet said anything to Terry about his plans.

As she lay in bed that night, Dana knew that Terry wouldn't object to going to the farm permanently. She couldn't expect any support from him when she tried to tell Bass they weren't going there to live. For a change, however, she was able to prevent herself from dwelling on it. Knowing Terry had been returned to her as Bass had promised, Dana fell into an exhausted dreamless sleep.

# Chapter Nine

During the following day there were moments when Dana remembered Bass's bizarre marriage proposal, but those moments were brief. She hoped that her life would go back to normal — there was no indication that Bass would ever see her again. All her worrying and soul searching had been for nothing. Apparently he had changed his mind.

Late in the afternoon the private line on her desk rang. Dana was immediately alarmed when she recognized Edith's voice because her friend never called unless there was an emergency.

"Dana, I think you had better come home."

"Terry?" she asked anxiously, thinking something must have happened to him.

"He isn't hurt or anything like that. Please, can you come home soon? We can't discuss it over the phone."

"I will be there as soon as I can."

Dana hung up the phone as she stood up and started around her desk. Her phone rang again but she ignored it as she reached for her purse and hurried out of her office. She quickly told her secretary there was an emergency at home and practically ran out the door.

The drive to her cottage seemed endless. Her imagination ran wild, coming up with all sorts of things that could have happened. As soon as she parked the car she hurried into the house and could hear Edith and Terry in the living room. Terry looked up at Dana as she came in and ran to her.

He seemed puzzled and confused as he hugged her tightly but Dana was relieved to see that he was all right.

"What's the matter?" She looked from Terry to Edith and back to the boy. "What is it?"

Edith ordered, "Come and sit down, Dana. Terry, let go of your sister so she can sit down."

When Dana was seated on the couch, Edith glanced with sadness in her eyes at Terry. "Terry and I were sitting on the patio when the phone rang and as usual Terry ran to answer it. When he returned, he looked strange so I asked him who was on the phone. Terry, you tell Dana what you told me."

At first the boy didn't look like he wanted to say anything but Dana ruffled his hair and said quietly, "Who was on the phone, Terry?"

Terry looked down at his bare feet. "The man on the phone said he was Mr. Ravenel and he wanted to leave a message for you. I knew it wasn't Bass. I could tell by his voice. I told him you were at work and he said he knew that. He was going to leave a message with the housekeeper. Then he asked who I was so I told him I was Terry Donatus. I even had to repeat my name because he didn't seem to understand what I said."

Dana's face had gone pale as she looked at her brother. She sighed, "Go on. What else did he say?"

"After he found out who I was, he asked me how old I was and when I told him, he . . . got mad. He swore and said something about you thinking *he* was a . . . a bastard. Then he laughed . . . a horrible laugh and said to tell you a check would be in the mail and he hoped it would be enough to make you change your mind about the . . . merger you had planned. What did he mean?"

Dana closed her eyes and leaned back against the couch.

Terry looked up at her. "He wanted to know if Bass knew me and I told him yes."

"Did he say anything else after that?"

He nodded. "He said to tell you not to try

that old trick and then hung up. Why was he so angry at me? I don't even know him. Isn't it all right for Bass to come here? I like him."

She looked at his young bewildered face and felt a protective urge to hold him against her and soothe away his fears. But he was no longer a small child. The time had passed when she could kiss the hurt to make it better.

"Mr. Ravenel is just mistaken about a few things, Terry."

"Is he related to Bass?"

"Yes. He is Bass's father." Looking at the face that was a younger version of Bass's, Dana's heart tightened in her chest. She had never been so close to telling the truth to her half brother. It would be so easy to say, "And he is your father, too," but she knew she couldn't do it.

The boy's head lowered. "He doesn't seem to like me much."

Dana glanced at Edith. She drew a deep breath and brought her gaze back to her brother. Somehow she had to allow him to go back to his carefree world of being a kid again, away from the intrigues and riddles of an adult world. He would learn about them soon enough.

She forced her voice to be calm. "Terry,

there is nothing for you to worry about. I'll take care of Mr. Ravenel. He won't bother you again. Just forget about everything he said. You have done nothing wrong."

"Are . . . are you going to tell Bass what his father said?"

"Oh yes," she stated with a hint of steel in her voice. "I'm going to tell Bass."

Terry gave her a tentative smile. "I guess Bass won't let his father talk to me that way again, will he?"

"If Mr. Ravenel calls again, I'll talk to him. You go out and play now."

"Okay." A look of relief flooded the tense, young face. He was again secure that his sister would take care of everything.

Dana only wished she could feel the same confidence in her ability to take care of problems.

At eight o'clock that evening the phone rang in the cottage. Dana got up from her chair, took the few steps between her chair and the table where the phone sat, and stared down at the phone as it continued its repetitious ringing.

Terry came to the door of his room and stood there watching her. She could hear the television set in his room mumbling in the background. Edith came out of the kitchen and stood near the entranceway.

After looking at each of them briefly, Dana answered the phone.

Bass's deep voice penetrated the silence in the room. "Dana, what is going on? I've been trying to get in touch with you all afternoon. I called your office and your secretary said you had left because of a family emergency. Then all I got was a busy signal from your home phone. Has anything happened to Terry?"

"I had the phone off the hook."

"For God's sake, why? Is Terry all right?"

"Yes."

Bass was getting impatient with her answers. "Why did you have the phone off the hook?"

"Why are you calling?" she countered.

There was a long pause before he said quietly, "What's wrong?"

"Nothing."

"The hell there isn't. What is going on?" he demanded.

If Terry hadn't been listening to the conversation, there was a lot she would have said but she was limited in how much she could say at the moment.

When she didn't respond to his question, he said her name angrily.

"Your father called here today. Terry answered the phone. J.P. knows . . ."

"Knows what?" asked Bass impatiently.

"What I didn't want him to know."

"Terry?" he asked in a tight voice.

"Yes."

"He hasn't said anything to me so maybe he doesn't know as much as you think."

She was trying to remain calm but it wasn't easy. "I won't have him calling here and upsetting Terry. J.P. was angry and said he thinks it's a trick . . . that I was trying to . . . pressure you into . . . you know what."

Rather grimly, Bass replied, "I'll talk to him." Then as if talking to himself, he added, "He didn't tell me he had called you when we talked about you at dinner."

Something snapped in Dana and she exploded, "Just forget the whole thing, Bass. From now on just leave me alone. Leave *us* alone."

There was a long silence, broken finally by Bass. "I can't do that, Dana."

"Well, you had better try because I've had it with both of you."

"We have plans, remember? Nothing has changed. You are going to marry me."

"You had the plans, not me."

"Dana, for God's sake. Calm down."

She answered in a way that said more than any words she could have spoken. She hung up the phone.

As if he knew better than to say anything to his sister right then, Terry went back into his room and shut his door. Edith left the doorway and came toward Dana, who had gone over to the cabinet to pour herself a drink. The sound of the bottle clanking against the glass brought Edith over to Dana. Edith poured a generous amount into the glass and held it out to Dana.

"Drink this. Come on. You're as pale as a ghost."

The brandy coursed through her veins, warming her and helping her gain her composure. She was still feeling a little shaky as she walked over to the couch. She gave a poor imitation of a laugh. "Remember our quiet evenings sitting by the fire when our biggest problem was whether we should get the roof fixed first or the screen door?"

Nodding her head, Edith said, "As it is, we never did get either one fixed."

"Yes, well, at least those problems are easier to solve." She added rather heatedly, "Damn those Ravenels."

"Dana, I'm disappointed in you."

Dana's head snapped up, surprised at the hard tone of Edith's voice.

Sitting on the edge of her chair, Edith stated flatly, "If you mean you would rather spend your evenings sitting with an old woman the rest of your life instead of with a man you care for, then you are not the woman I thought you were. And don't tell me you don't have strong feelings for that man — you wouldn't react this way unless you did. You will find life much more exciting and fulfilling with Mr. Bass Ravenel than hiding away from people by shutting yourself up in this house."

Dana could only stare at Edith. It was as if the tooth fairy had suddenly turned into a dragon.

"Edith, he wants to marry me, take Terry, and live at Ravenel Farms. All of us. He said by marrying me, Terry will become a Ravenel legally and take his rightful place as one of J.P.'s heirs. How can I marry a man I just met and live with him under those conditions? And J.P. . . . my God, Edith, to live in the same house . . . I can't do it."

Edith continued relentlessly, "It appears to me you are putting all of the blame on J.P. Ravenel again, just like you did eight years ago. He may deserve some of the blame but not all of it. Don't get me wrong, Dana," she said when she saw the hurt expression on Dana's face. "I'm not saying what he has done in the past is right but you have let what happened so long ago grow all out of proportion."

"That has nothing to do with Bass's plans," said Dana hastily. "J.P. is only part of it. What Bass is suggesting is impossible."

"You are judging Bass by his father's actions." At Dana's look of disbelief, Edith added, "Yes, you are. But remember Bass could also judge you by your mother's actions. After all she was involved with his father voluntarily. No one forced her to do what she did."

Dana sat numbly on the couch, a little shocked to face the bald facts Edith was hurling at her in rapid succession.

And she wasn't through yet. "I've met Bass only three times but he appears to me to be the type of man who is quite capable of taking care of you and Terry *and* his father, if you allow him to try."

Edith stood up and leaned over to put her hand on Dana's shoulder. "I want you to think over what I have said and see if I'm not right. My being here with you and Terry has been a substitute for companionship and security, but you need a fuller life with a man and a father figure for Terry." She paused briefly before she asked gently, "How do you feel about Bass Ravenel?"

Dana's bewildered eyes looked up. "I don't really know. So much has happened in such a short time."

"What if you could eliminate the thought of J.P. when you thought of Bass? Try to think of Bass as a man and not the son of J. P. Ravenel. You aren't like your mother. Why do you think Bass is like his father just because they have the same last name?"

Disturbed, Dana got to her feet and paced the floor. "It's not that easy."

Patiently, Edith stated, "I didn't say it was going to be easy, just that you should try."

"What about his feelings for me? I don't like the idea of marrying a man just so my brother can take his proper place as a Ravenel."

"Why don't you ask him about his feelings for you?"

The curtain of Dana's hair fell forward as she lowered her head and murmured, "I might not like the answer."

"Well, I'm going to leave you. I think you have some serious thinking to do." Edith moved toward her room. At the door, she turned. "Just be fair, Dana. To yourself and to Bass."

Dana stood still for a moment. Then she reached for her jacket hanging by the door and went outside into the darkness. She walked down toward the water, stepping carefully among the rocks. The closer she came to the water, the cooler the breeze became. She zipped up her jacket and shoved her hands into the pockets.

When she came to the beach, Dana sat down to remove her shoes. Clasping her knees, she dug her toes into the still-warm sand though the sun had set an hour before. The surface of the lake was like a piece of blue-black velvet undulating as if a fan were blowing gently underneath it. She never tired of watching the waves as they flowed across the beach for a short span then receded into the security of the lake.

She lay back on the sand with her arms behind her head and looked up at the clear sky, watching the tiny stars wink down at her. Edith's words echoed through her mind, and she had to admit that part of what the older woman had said was true. From the very first time she had seen Bass, she had thought of him as one of the hated Ravenels and it had prejudiced her thinking since then. Maybe it was wrong to let the past influence her now.

Time went by swiftly with deep reflection putting painful memories into their proper place. A maturity of thought and a ripening of spirit were replacing needless guilt and hate. Whatever the future held, she was at last free to see it untainted by the dusky screen of long ago.

Later as she let the shower wash away the sand, she still felt apprehensive about Bass's plans for her and Terry. Even if she was willing to meet J.P. halfway in an effort to make peace, his attitude so far wasn't exactly encouraging.

As she toweled herself dry, she couldn't help wondering what Bass was thinking about hearing her rant and rave over the phone. It was possible he no longer planned to carry out his threats to take her and Terry to the farm.

She slipped her favorite short white nightgown over her head and slid between the sheets. Her eyes closed but a vision of dark hair, dark eyes, and a tall virile body made it difficult to surrender to the waiting arms of sleep. In that drowsy state of semiconsciousness before she succumbed entirely to deep sleep, she had the vague desire to feel Bass's arms around her, to feel his mouth against hers, and to feel his warmth and strength near her.

At first she thought she was still dreaming when she felt a draft as the covers were pulled back and familiar hands were shaking her awake as a deep soft voice called her name. "Dana, wake up."

Her eyes half-opened but all she could see was a shadowy form bending over her. Subconsciously she must have known who it was because she wasn't afraid, although if she could have seen his expression, she might have been.

"What do you want?" she asked sleepily.

"I want to talk to you. Get up. We'll go outside so we don't disturb the boy."

The lamp on the bedside table was turned on and she opened her eyes further to watch him go to her closet. He moved several hangers along the pole until he came to her trench coat. He tore it off the hanger and threw it on the bed.

"Put that on. It's cold outside."

Suddenly she was aware of how little she had on. "Turn around first."

His impatience came through in his harsh undertone. "Just put it on, Dana. I have a general idea of what a woman looks like. You won't shock me."

Her lips tightened. She would have argued with him about coming into her bedroom at this time of night but he had reminded her that Terry's bedroom was right next to hers. If she was going to find out what he was doing here, she would have to do as he said and go outside with him.

He stood by her door waiting for her to put the coat on. After she belted it tightly around her, he steered her through the door.

It was chilly outside compared to the warmth of her bedroom and she shivered slightly. His strong hand grasped her elbow and he led her toward his car.

She held back. “I’m not going anywhere with you.”

“We are just going to sit in the car. It’ll be warmer.” His hand on her shoulder pressed her into the car. “Quit stalling, Dana. I’m not in the mood for it.”

After he was seated behind the wheel, there was an uncomfortable silence. Dana huddled against the door waiting for him to say something. Now that he had her exactly where he wanted her, he didn’t seem to be in any hurry to talk. Her watch was on the bed-side table and she had no idea how late it was. He could have waited until the morning when she was rested and would have felt more like facing him.

A thought suddenly came to her. She turned her head and looked at his profile. “How did you get into the cottage?”

Without looking at her, he answered, “Your door was unlocked. I hope you haven’t made a habit of being that careless.”

She replied tightly, “I’ll make sure from now on that the door is securely locked. You never know who might just walk in.”

She saw his jaw tighten as he stared

straight ahead. "You can be glad I could get in to you so easily. The way I feel I would have battered down the door."

Rather wearily, she asked, "What do you want, Bass?"

His arm rested on the steering wheel as he half turned in the seat to face her. His other arm lay on top of the seat, his hand only a few inches away from her shoulder. His voice was oddly strained, "Do you enjoy putting me through the wringer?"

Her head jerked around. "What are you talking about?"

"You have a nasty habit of hanging up the phone when I'm talking to you. It's just as well I was far away from you. I could have wrung your neck."

"It's clear your male ego can't take a little rejection. I thought that was plain enough. Why can't you take a hint? I didn't want to talk to you then and I'm not too wild about talking to you now."

His scowl could be seen in the moonlight. "That's too bad. I haven't driven all this way for nothing. We are going to get a few things straight between us . . . and there won't be any chance for you to stop it this time."

Part of Dana's irritation was due to her appearance. Why couldn't he have come when her hair was combed and she was dressed in clothes instead of her nightgown and her old trench coat? "Well, say what you came to say, then, so I can go back to bed."

His eyes remained on her face but for a long time he didn't speak. Finally when she was about to repeat her request, he spoke quietly, "I've been to see a lawyer. I started inquiries on adoption proceedings so Terry can become a Ravenel legally. The lawyer needs to see a copy of your guardian papers."

Dana sat in stunned silence. The pain was so intense and her anger so severe, she could hardly breathe. Her composure was shattered. She had had enough of words, meaningless words. Her hand went to the door latch but his hand shot out and grabbed her arm before she could open the door.

"Damn it, Dana. Where do you think you're going?"

"Away from you. Away from lies and fairy tales," she said in a shaking voice.

He grabbed her shoulder with a hard pressure that made her cry out with pain as he turned her around to face him. "I haven't told you any lies. Whatever you have dreamed up in that over-active mind of yours, you can just forget. You are not running away from me again. We are going to get a few things ironed out if it takes all night." His fingers eased their hold a little. "Now what is this about me telling you lies?"

"You are going to take Terry from me. All that about trust and you go right ahead and decide to adopt him and take him away."

He spoke very slowly, his voice quiet and a little restrained as if he was trying very hard to be patient. "If I am taking both of you to the farm, how do you figure I'm taking him away from you?"

"You . . . you just said you were going to adopt Terry. I . . . thought you had changed your mind about marrying me and were going to adopt Terry instead."

He looked closely at her, his eyes never leaving her face. "And that upset you? I thought you were fighting the idea of marrying me?"

She couldn't say anything for fear she would tell him how she felt about him. She lowered her head, her hair falling forward to shield her face.

His voice was slightly strained, phrasing his words as if he were talking to a rather stubborn child. "Dana, you will take my name when we are married but Terry's name has to be changed by a court. That is why I went to the lawyer to see what had to be done legally."

Dana slumped in the seat, exhausted with so many emotions pulling at her in all directions in such a short time. "I'm a fool."

She heard him chuckle. "I agree with you." He pulled her over toward him until she was half lying across his lap with the steering wheel at her back.

His head lowered and he touched her lips with his own, gently at first, then when she pressed closer to him, he tightened his hold and the tenderness became a burning pressure. Her body began to tremble as she slipped into a pool of sensual delight. When he pulled away from her, his face was all shadows and shapes in the darkness but Dana could see a hint of a smile. His voice was incredibly soft and husky as he said, "We always seem to have this."

She misunderstood him and stiffened. In her mind flashed J.P.'s nasty expression as his eyes had roamed up and down her body, smirking at her as he insinuated the attraction she held for Bass.

"Now what?" he asked impatiently.

She was unaware of the look of confusion in her eyes. "Is sex the only reason you are marrying me?" She added, "Other than for Terry's sake?"

He could feel her waiting for his answer as he stroked the satin soft skin along her throat. His hand slid down her neck until it rested on her bare shoulder under the thin strap of her nightgown while his thumb traced a soothing, sensual pattern.

"It's a part of the reason. Wanting you is a damn good reason to marry you." His lips caressed the sensitive spot on her throat where his hand had been. "And I want you very badly at the moment."

She swallowed nervously, "I'm . . . not experienced with men, Bass. You . . . may be disappointed."

His warm breath brushed her heated skin. "I'll take that chance."

"But marriage seems a pretty drastic step just to . . ." She couldn't say it. He lifted his head and Dana saw the smile of amusement on his mouth. She continued awkwardly, "Your father said you should have an affair with me and get me out of your system."

To her astonishment, he laughed. Oddly enough, his laughter made his father's words harmless. It gave a different slant to J.P.'s cruel innuendoes, making it seem ridiculous to take them seriously.

Bass murmured drily, "I think we can manage without Daddy's advice." He lifted her up a little and asked, "Now tell me about J.P.'s call and why it upset you."

Taking a deep breath, Dana told him what

had been said and also Terry's reaction to the call. She saw Bass's mouth tighten when she explained that J.P. thought Terry was a trick to get Bass to marry her. "He knows Terry can't be your son. We'll never get by with pretending he is. You were in Europe that summer."

He had been looking out the window as she was relating what his father had said to her but now he brought his gaze back to her, his eyes serious. "Dana . . ."

She knew then. But the knowledge didn't frighten her as much as it would have a week ago. "You told him the truth."

He nodded. "After you hung up the phone on me, I was boiling mad. I was in a hurry to get here and talk to you so I didn't go into much detail. J.P. said everything he could in an effort to make me give up the idea of marrying you. He told me how you broke the Commandment pencil and even how you tried to kill him. But having heard the background of the story from your point of view, not even that could sway me.

"My forgiveness, which is complete and unconditional, is not for the Dana Donatus who is with me right now, but for a sixteen-year-old girl whose family and life style were demolished all too suddenly. You desperately needed a scapegoat, and my father was the obvious choice.

"We may not have known each other for very long, but I'd have to be blind in order to overlook the absolute, untarnished goodness that radiates from you."

Dana stared unseeing into the night, though his words and their implications penetrated her heart as well as her mind. Both of them were unaware at that moment how much Bass was revealing to Dana about himself.

"I ended up giving him an ultimatum," Bass continued. "Either you and Terry will live at Ravenel Farms under the conditions I've set, or we will live somewhere else. I've left him with a lot to think about." His fingers combed through her hair distractedly. "I feel a certain responsibility toward him, Dana. After all, he is my father. He's not well, and he is frightened because of that. But I told him that I knew exactly what I was doing and that he would have to accept the situation."

Quietly, Dana stated, "I don't like being in the position of coming between you and your father."

He held her hand so that their fingers were interlaced and answered firmly, "I have to give him time to adjust to the whole situation, but it will all work out. In fact just before I left the house, he said, 'No wonder she hates me,' so at least he seems to be looking at it from a point of view other than his own."

"What about Terry?"

He looked puzzled. "What about him?"

"The fact that he looks so much like you may occur to him someday."

"You mean someone may say something to him?"

"It could happen."

He shrugged. "If it does, we'll talk about it and explain everything to him. He may not take it so badly that he is a Ravenel." He smiled faintly, "Remember, I'm the guy who brought champagne to his canoe launching. That is a point in my favor. And I'd like my father to get to know him."

Dana shivered in the cool night air and Bass wrapped her coat around her shoulders. She asked, "Are you . . . still going to adopt him? I mean, J.P. knows the truth now."

"I'm still going to adopt him."

"In what way? As your brother, your son, your ward?"

"I'll be his guardian along with you. That way Terry will have both of us legally responsible for him." His eyes narrowed. "You aren't fighting me anymore. You have accepted it.

You aren't giving me any objections about the adoption or the marriage. Why?"

She smiled shakily. "I'm adjusting."

He seemed disappointed in her answer but all he said was, "That's a start anyway." He lifted her off his lap until she was sitting in the seat next to him. "Let's go back inside. I could do with a cup of coffee."

The kitchen was warm but Dana kept her coat on rather than take it off and have only her brief nightgown covering her. Bass sat down in a chair, leaning it back against the wall, watching her as she moved around between the counter and the cupboards, getting out the cups and saucers and measuring coffee.

"Do you want anything to eat?" she asked as she switched on the coffee pot.

"No. I'm not hungry . . . for food."

Dana glanced quickly at him but just as quickly away again when she saw the glint in his eye and the crooked smile on his lips. She wished he had wanted something to eat so she could keep busy preparing food while the coffee was perking.

"Dana?"

She turned back and their eyes met for a long electric moment. She took an instinctive step toward him and then stopped in indecision.

He said gently, "Don't stop. Come here."

She moved slowly in his direction. He reached out and pulled her onto his lap, his arms coming around her.

"Dana, will you marry me?" he asked softly. "I haven't asked you properly before. I am now."

Her fingertip traced one of the buttons on his silk shirt, her eyes remaining fixed on the button as she avoided his intent look. Rather breathlessly she murmured, "You never asked me at all. You ordered."

"Hmm. I guess I did." His hand moved to stop her fingers. "I'm asking now. I'm asking you to trust me, to take my name, to live with me."

She then raised her eyes to meet his. He still hadn't said he loved her. But maybe her love would be enough and he would come to care for her someday. She had to take that chance. "Yes, Bass. I'll marry you."

She felt him let his breath out slowly as if he had been holding it waiting for her answer. He moved his head until his lips touched hers lightly. "I think that deserves a reward." He reached into his pocket and handed her a velvet covered box.

Opening the box, Dana gasped when she saw the brilliant emerald ring. Small diamonds surrounded the square-cut stone set in gold. When he had handed her the case, she knew it would contain a ring but not a ring like this. It must have cost a fortune. "Bass, I'd be afraid to wear it."

He smiled down at her. He took the ring out of the box and slipped it onto her finger. "Well, you'll just have to get used to it because it stays there."

"Am I ever going to be able to win an argument with you?" Dana asked in a bemused fashion.

His arms slipped under the coat and encircled her warm, pliant body. "You have weapons to win any battle we might have in the future. God help me when you discover how to use them."

His kiss was hungry and impatient, but he eventually was able to draw on his dwindling reserves of control and pull back from her. "Let's forget the coffee. Leave J.P., Terry, and anything else your over-active mind can worry about and let's go to bed."

"Bass . . ."

He looked at her face and grinned. "I'll take the couch and you go back to your room — alone — this time."

She levered herself off his lap. "I'll get you a blanket and a pillow."

"You could have at least put up a fight, sweetheart. I do have a reputation for being fairly adequate in the bedroom," he teased, his eyes sparkling.

She looked at him seriously, her feelings out in the open for him to see. "I might lose that fight too."

He looked long and hard at her and then smiled, "Go to bed."

# Chapter Ten

The alarm clock rang at six in the morning and Dana automatically reached over to push the button to silence it. Even though it had been late before she had finally gotten to bed, she woke quickly.

She showered and dressed in record time, anxious to see Bass again to make sure she hadn't dreamt that he had been there last night. She ran a comb through her hair and tied it back with a lime green ribbon that matched the lime green of her knitted top. She smoothed her navy skirt over her hips and slipped into the navy jacket of her suit as she headed for the door of her bedroom.

As she went through the living room on the way to the kitchen, she saw that Bass was still asleep on the couch. She took in his features, noticing how much younger he looked in his sleep. The couch was barely adequate for his long frame.

Stepping quietly through the room she went into the kitchen and found Edith cooking breakfast. On the stove were pans of sausages, bacon, and fried potatoes. A bowl of fresh eggs was waiting on the counter near the stove.

Pouring a cup of coffee for herself, Dana asked, "Are we expecting an army this morning?"

"Someone left the coffee pot plugged in all night. Would you know anything about that?" Edith returned drily.

"Guilty. You didn't answer my question."

Edith smiled. "Judging by the lump on the couch, I decided a bigger breakfast than usual would be required."

A deep voice growled from the doorway, "I resent being called a lump."

Both women turned toward the doorway where Bass stood. His hair was uncombed and a shadow of beard darkened his jawline. His hand tucked the shirttail of his wrinkled shirt into the waistband of his jeans. "I should warn you, Dana. Before I've had my cup of coffee, I bite little girls who look as bright and wide awake as you do this early in the morning."

Edith gently pushed Dana in the direction of the coffee pot. "For heaven's sake. Give him a cup of coffee before he becomes violent."

"An understanding woman," he mumbled. He came into the room and pulled out a chair so he could sit at the table. Dana set a cup of coffee in front of him and backed away in mock alarm.

"Are you always so grouchy in the morning?" she asked with a smile.

"Hmmm," was the only sound from him as he drank his hot coffee, his eyes on her over the cup. When he set the empty cup on the table, he rubbed his rough jaw. "I don't suppose there would be a razor around I could use?"

"I'll get you one." Dana went into her bathroom and reached into the wall cabinet for the razor. She set it by the sink and heard the door open a little further as Bass entered. He reached out for her, bringing her up against his hard body.

"Good morning."

She reached up and rubbed her hand against his jaw. "Is this what I'm going to have to face every morning over the breakfast table?"

She heard him murmur against her ear, "I'll shave three times a day." Then he leaned back to look down at her. "What makes you think you won't have to face me earlier than the breakfast table? Married people sleep together as a general rule."

A faint shadow entered her eyes. "Most people marry for normal reasons. You can't say our reasons are exactly normal."

His arms fell to his side. He went to the sink and turned on the faucet. "Our reasons may not be the normal ones but our marriage will be."

Rather thoughtfully, Dana closed the door as she left the bathroom. A slight frown creased her forehead. Bass seemed angry about something. Maybe he was one of those people who are naturally cranky in the morning.

Back in the kitchen, Edith was stirring the sausages to prevent them from scorching. She looked up from her task as Dana came into the room. "Well?"

"Well, what?"

Edith asked patiently, "Is the situation clearer today than yesterday?"

Dana shrugged, "In some ways." Looking around the room, she said, "Is there anything I can do to help? You've gone to an awful lot of trouble this morning."

Edith gave her a sharp glance. "You can butter the toast. I have a feeling he will demand to be fed when he discovers a human being looking back at him in the mirror."

A squeal of young laughter came from the area of the bathroom. Terry had discovered Bass.

Edith commented, "To be a child again. Terry accepts Bass's presence without question. To him it's a natural event."

Together they dished up platters of food and set the table. Edith set the juice glasses at each plate and then stood back to admire the results. As if to herself, she muttered, "Needs something," then went outside. She was back shortly with a single rose in her hand. When the flower was placed in a crystal bud vase and positioned in the middle of the table, she smiled with approval.

Dana moved to stand near her friend. "You like him, don't you?"

Edith's expression was faraway. "He reminds me of my late husband at times. Frank was a wonderful man with special qualities until . . . until he became ill. He always insisted that a big breakfast was the best way to get a day started."

Surprised, Dana stared at the woman. "I didn't know you had been married, Edith."

Edith replied, "It was a long time ago."

"And you don't want to talk about it?" asked Dana carefully. Though she was a little hurt that her friend had not confided in her, Dana completely understood the emotional need for discretion.

"Not really."

After a brief hesitation, Dana blurted out, "Edith, Bass asked me to marry him. I . . .

have agreed to marry him."

"I can't say I'm too surprised. Relieved, but not surprised."

"He said we will be living at Ravenel Farms. You will come with us, won't you, Edith?" Her serious voice changed to light humor. "I have the feeling it will take both of us to tame Bass Ravenel to a domestic life."

The two women looked at each other with affection, knowing that a period in each of their lives had ended but another phase was about to begin.

Edith patted Dana's hand and said cryptically, "We'll talk about it later."

Breakfast was eaten, mostly by Bass and Terry with Edith and Dana acting like indulgent nannies supervising the antics of their charges. Bass told funny stories and teased Terry, making them all laugh throughout the meal.

Dana hated to end the most carefree breakfast they had ever had, but she had to go to work. When she mentioned it, Bass told her he would drive her to the Village. He wanted to go shopping for a change of clothes and then he would come to take her out to lunch. He also told her there would be a meeting between himself, Dana, and Elliott at eleven o'clock.

"Whatever for?" Dana asked.

Bass grinned broadly. "To discuss your resignation and invite him to the ceremony. We have an appointment with the Justice of the Peace two weeks from tomorrow."

Terry was confused and looked from one adult to the other. "But why? We didn't do anything wrong."

Bass grinned down at him. "We are going to do something right. Your sister is going to marry me."

Terry let out an excited yell. "Are we going to live at your place?"

"Yes. We'll be going there in two weeks. You can start packing the things you need for a few days as soon as we get back from shopping if you want. I'll have most of your belongings brought out to the farm."

"The canoe too?" asked Terry anxiously. "I could use it on the pond I saw the other day."

"Of course, the canoe must come too. I wouldn't think of leaving it behind."

Edith, after glancing at Dana's white face, said, "Terry, let's go check to see how clean your hands and face are."

"But I . . ." he protested.

Edith insisted, "Come on, young man."

When they were alone, Bass put his hands on Dana's shoulders. "You did say you would marry me, Dana."

Her eyes looked up at him with a bewildered expression in their depths. "But so soon?"

His eyes narrowed slightly. "Does it matter when?"

"It's so sudden."

"I've got the license and we have plenty of time to get the blood tests."

Her eyes pleaded with him. "But what is the hurry? We have plenty of time. Can't I — we — get used to the idea and eventually, after we get to know each other better, get . . . married?" She knew she was babbling but she was fighting panic. It was one thing to discuss a marriage that would take place in the distant future but quite another to go through with it.

"What about my job? I can't just leave without being sure that Elliott has had time to find someone to take my place."

"We can discuss that at eleven o'clock."

"But . . ." she protested.

His eyes pinned her to the spot, as if he was trying to determine how strong her objections really were. "I don't have a lot of time, Dana. I have work to do at the farm. Besides," he added softly, "I don't think I can wait much longer than two weeks, and you did say you trusted me."

"I . . . do."

He chuckled and kissed her nose. "Remember those words."

She smiled tremulously, still confused. "I seem to have lost control of my own life. Two weeks ago I didn't even know you and now . . ."

His face became serious, his voice firm, almost severe. "Do you want to change your mind? This will be for keeps once we are married, Dana."

She looked at him steadily. Bass Ravenel was practically a stranger. He had the name she had hated for so many years. His father would be living in the same house. Her whole life had been turned upside down by this man but she was sure of one thing . . . her life would never be dull. It was simple. She needed him. It was unbelievable, a bit mad, but somehow she was going through with it.

Keeping her expression solemn, she said seriously, "I must tell you one thing."

She felt his tension. "What is it?"

"I sure hope I'll have enough time to find a suitable dress."

He pulled her against him roughly as his mouth fastened onto hers. The kiss was almost a punishment for giving him a bad moment, but delicious, stirring punishment. They clung to each other violently, as if daring anything in the world to pry them apart.

"Oh God, Dana," he growled. "I thought you were going to change your mind."

Her arms remained locked around his neck as she took a tiny step backward. "Are *you* sure?" she asked. "Don't marry me if it is only because you desire me and want to give Terry a name. I . . . I want more than that out of my life."

He sighed, "I've never been more sure of anything. It will work out, darling. Just give it a little time." He released her when he heard Terry returning to join them.

It wasn't long before Bass noticed that the boy had become unnaturally quiet and withdrawn. It was such a tentative, precarious situation — this getting to know Terry — and he had nothing to guide him except his instincts. His instinct now told him that the boy was feeling left out of the plans.

When he asked Terry to come along with him, he was rewarded with a broad grin on the young face.

Dana went up the stairs to her office after Bass had driven her to the Village. That morning, there were piles of letters on her desk, but her mind had a terrible time settling down to routine work.

A few minutes before eleven Dana was interrupted at her desk by the inter-office buzzer. It was Elliott asking her to come in to his office. When she opened her door, she saw Terry in one of the chairs in the reception area and went over to him.

"Why are you sitting out here?" Dana asked.

"Bass told me to wait for him so he could go talk to Elliott." He held up a thick book about boats so she could see the cover. "He bought me this book."

She read the title. *Sailing Vessels, Then and Now.* She smiled. "Very appropriate for you. Do you want to sit at my desk and read it? It looks heavy to be holding on your lap."

He nodded his head and did as she suggested.

She entered Elliott's office and immediately saw Bass sitting in one of the chairs across the desk from Elliott. Both men looked up as she came in.

Elliott indicated the chair next to Bass. "Have a seat, Dana. There has been a new development we should discuss."

Obeying her boss's instructions, Dana sat down next to Bass, glancing briefly in his direction. His shopping expedition had been successful. He wore a pair of dark brown slacks and a light tan shirt with dark brown pinstripes. A blazer that matched the pants was slung over the arm of the chair.

Elliott leaned back in his chair. "I've just been telling Bass about the strange phone call I got two days ago that concerns the pencil collection. A muffled male voice insisted that one of the pencils is a fake and asked for five thousand dollars to keep quiet about it."

With a quick glance toward Bass and then back to Elliott, Dana stated, "One of them *is* a fake."

Bass looked at her levelly. "That's not true. I didn't tell you this before — I only learned about it last night myself — but J.P. took the pieces of the pencil you broke and had it restored many years ago. The job was a tough one," he continued with a teasing grin in Dana's direction, "both halves were pretty badly splintered."

"I see," Dana said, wondering why that possibility had not occurred to her before. Perhaps, she thought, this was further evidence that her condemnation of the Ravenels and attitude toward the pencil collection were colored by emotion, were based on a desperate need to reject the existence of parental fallibility that she had been so harshly confronted with eight years before.

Then Elliott continued. "The telephone company was able to trace the call to the home of Theodore Way, a freelance curatorial consultant that Mr. Josef hired to help with the installation of the exhibit."

"That makes sense," Dana said under her breath. "Theodore was present on the day we unpacked the crates in the museum and I said there were only nine Commandment pencils."

"Yesterday morning," Elliott explained, "the police got a warrant and searched Mr. Way's apartment. Sure enough they found Polaroid photographs of the restored Commandment pencil along with a written statement that was clearly intended to be sent anonymously to members of the press. They also found a bottle of the same sleeping drug that had knocked out the guard the night you went to the museum."

"But why would Theodore do such a thing?" Dana asked. "He always seemed like such a nice young man."

"Yes, didn't he?" Elliott agreed sorrowfully. "Apparently Mr. Josef discovered that he had a history of embezzling funds from a museum where he worked on the East Coast. Instead of bringing this to my attention, Mr. Josef simply informed Theodore that our museum would no longer require his services. What this means, I suppose, is that the motivation for the crime is ultimately beyond my comprehension but is probably the result of a grave psychological disturbance."

After a weighty moment of silence, Bass spoke softly. "I must meet with my lawyers to discuss how to proceed. I have no choice other than to press charges."

"And what about Mr. Josef's error in judgment?" Dana asked. "He really should have advised us of the situation immediately."

"Mr. Josef is a pompous fool, but his heart is in the right place. I am sure that no drastic measures will be necessary," Elliott said, dismissing the issue with a wave of his hand.

Dana smiled at him warmly, her love and respect for Elliott reaching new heights.

"Enough unpleasant business for now," he continued, taking off his glasses and polishing them. "From what Bass tells me congratulations are in order." He slipped the glasses back on and met Dana's eyes. "Though I was more than a trifle surprised when I received your two weeks' notice this morning."

Startled, Dana asked, "What are you talking about?"

"You have just resigned from your position as assistant director."

"I . . . have?"

Elliott nodded. "It's official."

"Who said so?"

"Him," replied Elliott smoothly, pointing a long finger at Bass.

She slowly turned her head to meet Bass's amused eyes, shocked at his audacious infringement on her personal obligation. "You . . . you are —"

Bass said lazily, "What am I?"

She hesitated, searching for just the right word to wipe that smug look off his face but had to settle for the only one she could think of. "You're impossible."

Elliott laughed, "That's telling him off."

"She does have a way with words, doesn't she?" Bass asked.

Dana chose to ignore his remark and looked at Elliott seriously.

"I hope this will give you adequate time to find someone to take over my job. If necessary, I'm sure we can arrange —"

"— Dana, my dear, though you are unquestionably irreplaceable, I already know who I will ask to be the new assistant director."

Both Bass and Dana looked at him questioningly.

"It's Marion. She's been saying that she would like to go back to work, and with her methodical way of thinking and talent for working with people, she'll handle the job very well. I haven't mentioned it to her yet, but I'm almost sure she'll accept."

Dana was truly pleased about this turn of events. She liked her job very much and felt comfortable handing over her responsibilities to someone whose competence she trusted so enormously "That would be wonderful, Elliott," she said. "I'll need the rest of this week to sort out a few things, and — if Marion does opt to take over — I can start working with her next Monday if you like."

"That would be perfect, Dana," Elliott replied.

And so the meeting ended with good faith and cheerful anticipation of new beginnings.

The next two weeks passed quickly for Dana. At work there was a large number of projects to either complete or prepare for Marion, who had been delighted to accept the job. Dana's evenings were just as hectic — she had to go through Terry's and her own belongings to decide what was to be sent to Ravenel Farms and what was to be left behind.

She ended up working nonstop until noon on her wedding day. The ceremony was to be at five o'clock, and she hadn't even had time to shop for a dress. After leaving her office for the last time, Dana had lunch with Terry and Bass at a hamburger stand. Bass and Terry sat on one side of the wooden picnic table facing Dana. The hot noon sun was blotted out to some extent by the overhanging branches of a tree.

With a half-eaten hamburger in her hand, Dana teased, "You sure know how to treat a girl royally, Mr. Ravenel."

He smiled, "Blame Terry. It was his idea."

Terry happily took a bite from his hamburger and nodded his head enthusiastically, "It was a good idea, too."

When they were finished, Dana looked at her watch. "I must get back to town. Can we drop Terry home so I can pick up my car?"

"I will drive you wherever you need to go."

"Oh, no! I'm going shopping alone," Dana replied firmly. She was going to be nervous enough finding a dress for her wedding without having him along with her.

He didn't pursue it. "I have some running around to do before five o'clock anyway," he said, without going into detail. "Finish your lunch, Terry, then we'll go."

With a quick swipe across his face with a napkin, he picked up his wrappers and helped clear the rest of the table. Then he followed Bass and Dana to the car.

It wasn't long before Bass drove into the driveway of the cottage. He spoke over his shoulder to Terry, "You run on ahead, Terry. I want to speak to your sister for a moment."

Bass watched Terry as he ran into the cottage, banging the door behind him. He continued to stare out the window and Dana was beginning to wonder what he wanted to talk to her about. There was a strange tightness in her stomach. Had he changed his mind?

Finally he spoke, his voice quiet and steady. "Dana, there is something I'm curious about."

"What?"

His head turned and his sharp eyes found hers. "Will you be buying a white dress?"

A tint of pink appeared across her cheekbones. "Does it make any difference?"

A corner of his mouth rose. "Only in the way I make love to you. You'll just have to take my word for it. There is a difference. If you mean, would I change my mind about marrying you if you don't buy a white dress, the answer is no."

Dana's tongue wet her lips nervously, "I think we should discuss . . . that before we are married."

"By *that,* I take it you mean when we finally become man and wife in every way," he said with obvious amusement.

Choosing her words carefully, Dana declared, "We will be married in a rush but I don't think we need to rush into a more intimate relationship . . . at least not right away."

He gave her a probing glance. "When would you consider it the right time?"

She glared at him. He wasn't making this any easier. "I don't know. I just feel we should wait until we've known each other awhile."

"I didn't realize there was a time frame for two people who are attracted to each other to sleep together." His voice held a thread of sarcasm. "Live and learn." His hand rubbed his jaw in irritation. "This is a hell of a time to bring all this up."

"I think it is exactly the right time to bring it up," she said defensively. "It wouldn't be fair of me to go through the ceremony later today with you expecting more than I plan to give." She faced him with her chin tilted up defiantly, "Unless you want to change your mind now you know my condition to going through with this marriage."

He stared at her as if considering just how serious she was. His expression was unreadable as his eyes rested on her flushed cheeks.

When he didn't say anything, she said apprehensively, "Well, do you want to change your mind?"

His hand closed around the key in the ignition and he started the engine. He reached across her to open her door. "Go buy your dress, Dana. I'll pick you up at four-thirty."

It was her turn to stare at him. He hadn't answered her question exactly except to state the ceremony would continue . . . but what would he expect afterwards? She made no move to get out of the car. She had the sickening feeling she was making a fool of herself but she couldn't help it.

Finally he replied, his voice silky and smooth, a slight knowing smile curving his masculine mouth. "We'll try it your way . . . for a while. It will be interesting to see how long it will take before you give in to your passionate nature. If you think we can live under the same roof and sleep in the same bedroom without it going any further, I'll let you kid yourself as long as you can." His voice hardened slightly. "But I'm warning you, Dana. I won't wait forever. I don't plan on sacrificing the magic between us for some idiotic whim of yours for too long. I've wanted you from the first moment I saw you in that black bikini in your office. The thought that I hardly knew you didn't enter into it. When you can be honest with yourself and admit that you want me the same way, you'll have to let me know. Until then, I'll leave you alone."

With a gesture of his hand, he indicated for her to get out of the car. She pushed open thc door, feeling deflated and disappointed. What had she expected? She had made a condition and now she felt crushed that he had agreed to it. After she closed the door but before she walked away from the car, she heard him say her name. Leaning down to look through the open window, she saw his slow smile. "What?"

"You didn't answer my question."

Puzzled, she racked her brain to try to figure out what question he meant. To refresh her memory, he asked, "What color dress will you be buying?"

Exasperated, she snapped, "White."

He chuckled as he slipped the car into gear. "That's what I thought." With a wave of his hand, he said, "See you later."

Dana stood in the driveway watching the car back out, change gears, then drive away. Was she ever going to be sure of him? She frowned. Why should she expect to understand him? She didn't even understand herself. But one thing she did know — she was going to become Mrs. Bass Ravenel and try her damndest to make Bass want her for more than her body.

Dana was ready fifteen minutes early only because Edith had taken complete charge of her and Terry, coaxing and bullying them to make sure they were ready on time.

After trying on almost every white dress in Clear Lake, Dana chose a simply styled knee-length gown with a scoop neckline and gently tapered skirt. The material was silky with a lace pattern throughout, ending in a lacey scallop edging around the hem. She piled her hair up on top of her head but decided on wearing only the gold bracelet her father had given her on her fifteenth birthday. Nothing else had looked quite right so it was better to go without. The dress and shoes had made a sizeable dent in her bank account. She knew it wouldn't stretch to include a string of pearls.

Edith looked charming in a pink silk dress with lace trim and a pink hat with a small pheasant feather band. Terry was unusually neat in a grey suit, spotless white shirt, and grey tie. His windblown hair had been severely disciplined by prolonged combing. He was noticeably uncomfortable in his good clothes, yet excited about the wedding and going to live at Ravenel Farms.

Bass still hadn't arrived as Dana stood in front of the full-length mirror in her room studying her reflection. Edith was seated on the bed looking unusually serious. Dana caught the older woman's solemn expression in the mirror.

"Is there something on your mind, Edith?"

With a rather sheepish look on her face, Edith met Dana's eyes in the mirror. "I've been trying to find a way to tell you something."

Turning around, Dana came over and sat down beside Edith. "What is it? I hope you're not worried about me." She hoped her voice sounded more sure than she was. "I know what I'm doing."

With a gentle smile, the older woman reassured her, "It's not about your marriage. Bass will take good care of you and Terry."

"Then what is it?" Dana was becoming more and more concerned now.

"Oh dear. This is such a bad time to mention it. Right before your wedding and all. It's just that I know you were counting on me coming to Ravenel Farms with you and I'm going to have to disappoint you."

Clearly shocked, Dana could only stare at Edith for a long moment. Finally she managed to murmur, "But Edith, you know you'll be more than welcome there. You heard Bass say he expected you to come to the farm with us."

Edith patted her hand gently. "I know, I know. But I would like to stay here in the cottage if it is all right with you. I don't know what plans you and Bass have made for the cottage but I would like to rent it from you for awhile. I have my reasons for wanting to stay in Clear Lake."

Dana was so surprised by this sudden turn of events she was beginning to wonder if she knew anything at all anymore. "You can stay here as long as you want but I would like to know why . . . if you want to tell me."

There was a distant cloudiness in Edith's kind eyes. "It's because of Colby."

"Colby?"

"Colby Burris is my son."

Dana gasped in amazement, "Your son?"

"I started to work for your family when Colby was in school and we were living with my sister. My husband was in a mental institution at that time and I didn't think your family, especially your mother, would hire me if she knew I had a husband in an institution and that I also had a child." She turned toward Dana, saying sincerely, "I know it wouldn't have made any difference to you,

Dana, but since I started with a lie, I just continued to live that lie."

"But why didn't you tell me when we moved here?"

"Colby wanted to be on his own but I wanted him to be near me so when we moved to Clear Lake, he followed and got a job at the Village. He liked my sister's name of Burris and used that instead of his real name. It wouldn't have made any sense to tell anyone that he was my son, and besides, hiding our relationship had become second nature by then. Now that you will be leaving, I decided it was best if I stay near him. I want to be close in case . . . well, the doctors told me a long time ago that Colby could get progressively worse like . . . my husband did." She sighed. "You may have noticed that he is gentle and quiet, but not quite like other people in some ways — like his father."

Slipping her arm around the plump woman, Dana said quietly, "If you want to stay here, Edith, it is all right with me. I'll call you from Ravenel Farms to make sure you have everything you need. And we'll only be a two hour's drive away, so I'll expect you to visit often." She sighed heavily, "I'm going to miss you so much."

Responding with a hug, Edith said in a relieved tone, "I'll miss you, too, dear, but it's time for things to change. You don't need me anymore but my son does." She smiled. "I'm so pleased you have finally found someone like Bass Ravenel who will take care of you. I was beginning to wonder if you ever would settle down with a man and live a normal life."

They both heard the sound of a car outside. Dana replied grimly with some feeling, "I don't know how normal it's going to be but it certainly won't be boring. I'm having second and third thoughts about this whole thing."

Chuckling, Edith stood up. "That is just bridal nerves. Come along. I think your fiancé has arrived. We had better not keep him waiting."

Swallowing the lump in her throat, Dana murmured, "You go ahead. I have a few more things to do first."

When she was alone, Dana looked around the room that had been her sanctuary and haven for such a long time. Though most of her belongings were packed away, a bottle of her favorite perfume remained on her dresser. She absently sprayed some of the fragrance behind her ears and on her wrists. The security this room represented was about to be lost forever — everything and everyone seemed to be rotating in a confusing pattern of transformation until she wasn't sure she knew anything at all about the people around her.

She took a deep breath. Just this once she was going to follow her heart and not her head. She pulled herself upright, her pride straightening her spine. Somehow she would make him care for her. It wouldn't be easy. He was a man who followed his own path no matter how many obstacles were in his way. In fact her instinct told her that he was the type of man who rather enjoyed fighting for something he wanted. It made the prize all the more valuable.

She walked over to a still-open carton and gently removed a porcelain music box from its wrapping of crumpled newspaper. Her fingers found the catch and the tinkling sounds brought a tender smile to her lips. The melody was "Moon River," and she remembered the expectant look on Terry's face when he had given it to her for her birthday last year. Her smile faded. Terry was the reason Bass was marrying her. It was up to her to make him include her in his future plans.

She had one hold on him. He wanted her. He had made that clear more than once. She was a challenge to his male pride. As long as that challenge existed, she stood a chance in creating more of a bond between them than passion.

The door behind her opened. A quick glance in the mirror revealed the image of Bass entering her bedroom and closing the door softly behind him. With more perception than she had given him credit for, he asked, "Saying goodbye?"

She turned off the music box. "I suppose I am in a way." She turned to face him, taking in the devastating effect of the three-piece white suit he was wearing. He looked tall, tanned, and exceedingly handsome. "That's not fair. Everyone is supposed to be looking at the bride, not the groom."

His smile at her compliment reached his eyes. "You look beautiful and you know it." He held up a creamy white orchid. "I'll pin this on for you."

The back of his hand burned the skin on the upper rise of her breast as he slipped his fingers under the neckline of her dress so he didn't stick her with the long pin. The orchid was securely fastened to her dress but his hand remained against her flesh a fraction of a second longer than necessary as their gazes locked. His fingers moved to the cleft between her breasts.

"Your heart is racing," he said quietly. "Nerves?"

She licked her lips nervously, "I don't get married every day."

His eyes went to the spot where his fingers had been and then came back to her moistened mouth. "That's true. Are you sure it isn't for any other reason?"

Dana hadn't seen him move but he seemed so much closer to her. She could feel the heat of his body and inhaled the spicy scent of his after-shave as she took a steadying breath. He was so overpoweringly masculine and his nearness was torturing her. Some of her feelings were in her eyes as she searched his.

His voice was low and husky. "Don't look at me that way, sweetheart. That orchid crushes very easily, you know."

Strong hands at her waist didn't allow her to move away from him, but she managed to turn her head so she didn't have to look at him. He took advantage of the vulnerable throat exposed to his view and pressed his lips against the perfumed skin. "Poor baby," he murmured against her throat. "Fighting a battle with yourself when all you have to do is surrender in order to be the winner."

Dana's eyes closed as the intoxicating tremors flowed through her. She wanted him to kiss her and to go on kissing her until she was senseless and couldn't think. All her earlier resolves to keep her distance seemed ridiculous and childish compared to the delicious sensations only he could give her. With her last ounce of pride, she whispered, "We have a wedding to go to, remember?"

Bass raised his head. There were flecks of light in his dark eyes as he took in her flushed cheeks and dazed eyes. He was remarkably cool as he replied with a slight smile, "I remember." He took her hand. "Let's go make all this legal."

Edith and Terry sat in the back seat of Bass's car while Dana rode in the front beside Bass. She had no idea exactly where they were going and was surprised to see they were headed in the direction of Mason City. Soon they were driving through the city until Bass slowed the car and turned into the driveway of a church.

Her questioning eyes met his as he shut off the engine. "I thought . . ."

"I changed my mind," was all he said.

A little dazed by the altered plans, Dana walked beside Bass to the entrance of the church and was turned over to Edith when they were inside. Through a wide doorway, Dana caught a glimpse of Elliott and Marion sitting at the front of the church. Louise was seated next to Barbara behind them.

The minister was just coming out of a room located near the entrance when he saw her standing there. He introduced himself and asked her to go into the room he had just left. He opened the door and ushered her in saying she had ten minutes before the ceremony began and would be summoned in time. Bass gave her a last look before he walked away alongside the minister.

She entered the room. It was apparently the minister's office as there was a desk, several chairs, many books, and a large Bible opened on a stand against a wall. Near the desk was a man seated in a wheelchair. J. P. Ravenel.

As she stared at him, her heart sank and she cried silently, "Don't let him ruin my wedding."

"Dana, please sit down for a moment. I have only a few minutes to say what I feel must be said and it will be a little bit easier for me if you sit down."

Cautiously Dana moved toward the chair several feet away from him and lowered herself into it.

His voice was oddly hesitant, his face serious as he started to speak. "Dana, there isn't much time to go into a great deal of detail but I must say that I am sorry for the way we became acquainted eight years ago. I did care for your mother but not enough to leave her alone as I should have done. I cannot undo the things that happened . . . your father's death, the scene you interrupted between your mother and me —"

She made an impatient gesture and was about to protest when he lifted his hand imperiously to stop her.

"Let me finish. I don't expect a few words said now will erase all that's happened between us. I'm not proud of my past but your attitude then and recently has influenced my behavior toward you. Too many harsh words have been spoken by each of us, and we must try to forget them."

He paused for breath. "You will soon marry my son and come to live at Ravenel Farms. Because of that and because I love my son, I want to make my peace with you now. There are many things we have to discuss — my . . . other son is one of the more important things but this . . . disagreement between you and I must end first."

Dana knew it had required a great deal of courage on J.P.'s part to abase himself in front of her. He was a man of immense pride and she had a fair share of that commodity herself. He was right. They both loved Bass and for once they had a common bond to work from. J.P. also had a right to get to know Terry and to provide for him. If she was to have any chance to create a happy life with Bass, she would need to let go of her previous antagonism toward his father.

There was a tap at the door. Edith poked her head around the door. "Dana, it's time."

Dana stood, hesitated briefly, then walked up to J.P.'s chair. "J.P. — I don't have anyone to give me away. Would . . . would you?"

Amazement, relief, and pleasure all crossed his face as he stared up at his future daughter-in-law. In a choked voice, he replied, "I would consider it an honor."

A few moments later, Dana walked down the aisle to the tune of the wedding march played on an organ with J.P. in his wheelchair beside her. Terry was pushing the wheelchair from behind and they slowly approached the altar. It must have been quite an incongruous-looking wedding party but Dana knew it was the right thing to do. Especially when she saw the look on Bass's face as he watched them.

Later Dana signed her new name in the wedding book, her left hand with a gold ring on her third finger holding down the page. She was Mrs. Sebastion Ravenel.

# Chapter Eleven

The sun was a golden glow on the horizon by the time they were finally on the road to Ravenel Farms. Elliott had insisted on a small celebration after the ceremony and they had all gone to the Brass Rail Restaurant's private room for champagne and hors d'oeuvres.

In a way Dana had been relieved to have that extra time to get used to her new status as Bass Ravenel's wife. She was in familiar surroundings with friends who made it all seem natural and normal to be married to a man she had known for such a short time.

Elliott had kept everyone laughing by making outrageous remarks about married life punctuated by the occasional exasperated look from his wife. He finally made a serious toast to the bride and groom that brought a lump of emotion to Dana's throat. She felt like a fraud, duping her friends who all thought they had married for love.

As if he knew what she was thinking, Bass had laid his hand over hers where it rested on the table, his fingers playing with her wedding ring for a brief moment. His expression was solemn.

Now she leaned her head back against the leather upholstery, only half-listening to J.P. patiently answering the many questions Terry was asking about the farm. She was glad they had decided to change into comfortable traveling clothes for the long motor trip. Since Bass didn't seem inclined to talk to her, she gave in to the drowsy feeling that was making her lids heavy. Whether it was the champagne she had had earlier or nerves, she slipped into a light doze.

The absence of sound and motion wakened her. The car was parked in the drive in front of a large white house. Sitting up straighter, Dana noticed the front door was open but she couldn't see anything or anyone through the screen door.

They all had apparently gone into the house. She grimaced. She and the luggage had been left behind. Not a very encouraging beginning to her life at Ravenel Farms.

The heavy, humid night air was making Dana uncomfortable inside the car so she decided to get out. As she started walking to the house, the sound of the screen door slamming shut brought her eyes to the front porch. Bass came toward her, his long legs covering the distance quickly.

"So sleeping beauty finally woke up," he drawled. His smile partially soothed her irritation. "I was looking forward to waking you with a kiss."

She ignored that. There was a hint of annoyance in her voice. "I thought you had forgotten about me."

His smile faded. "I had to get J.P. out of this heat."

She felt a tension in him as he took her arm and escorted her into the house. As they entered, J.P. was allowing Terry to push his wheelchair as they went down the wide, brightly lit hall.

"If you wouldn't mind, Dad, how about you and Terry giving Dana a tour? I'll bring in the luggage." Bass gave Dana a long, unreadable look and went back outside.

Because of the wheelchair, the tour consisted of only the downstairs. But even so, that took a long time. It was a very large house. After they left the spacious living room, J.P. explained that the study had been converted into a bedroom for him since his illness made it difficult for him to use the stairs. They wandered through the den where there was a gun collection, displayed on one wall, that Terry had to point out to Dana. He also had to show Dana where the television was concealed behind a panel built into the wall. Terry had somehow taken over J.P.'s duties as tour guide and Dana saw the pleased look on the older man's face. Terry already felt very much at home here.

The next room was the dining room and Terry didn't linger there but practically dragged her into the kitchen to introduce her to the housekeeper, Mrs. Bird, who was helping the cook, Mrs. Schumacher. Both ladies beamed at Dana and welcomed her to Ravenel Farms. It was the first time Dana had been called Mrs. Ravenel and she hoped her face didn't register the shock she felt.

They ended up in the sun room. Floor-to-ceiling glass panels stretched across two walls and exposed a fantastic view of the surrounding countryside — what could be seen in the moonlight. The room showed signs of regular use. The colorfully patterned cushions on the white rattan furniture were comfortably worn. There was a bookmark sticking out of a thick mystery novel, and a variety of current magazines were piled up on the coffee table.

J.P. indicated that Terry and Dana were to sit down. "Mrs. Bird will call us when dinner is ready. We might as well be comfortable while we are waiting." When Dana was seated, he asked, "Well, Dana, what do you think of Ravenel Farms so far?"

She glanced briefly around the room. "You have a lovely home, J.P.," she replied politely. It *was* a beautiful house but she felt like a guest. She wondered how long it would be before she felt as if she belonged here.

A deep voice came from the doorway. "It's now your home, too, Dana."

They all turned to look at Bass. Dana got the impression he didn't care for her comment. Thankfully the awkward moment was interrupted by Mrs. Bird coming to the door to announce dinner.

During the meal, J.P. kept most of his attention on Terry. He seemed fascinated by the young boy now that he knew Terry was his son. When J.P. mentioned getting Terry a pony, he was rewarded with glowing enthusiasm, and Bass just smiled.

When she met Bass's amused eyes, she couldn't manage a smile in return. She couldn't get rid of the suffocating feeling of being an appendage. They had wanted Terry and therefore, had to take her as well. As Mrs. Bird served the meal cooked by Mrs. Schumacher, Dana also wondered what on earth she was going to do at

Ravenel Farms. The past two weeks had been so hectic that this hadn't occurred to her before. She wasn't needed to keep house or cook. In fact, she wasn't actually needed for anything.

Bass's amusement disappeared as he searched her face thoroughly. She looked down at her plate and continued to push the food around with her fork, occasionally taking a bite even though she had somehow lost her appetite.

As Mrs. Bird began to serve the dessert, Bass pushed his chair back and stood up. Speaking to his father, he said, "I'm going to show Dana the rest of the house. You and Terry go ahead and finish eating. We'll join you in the sun room later."

Without giving her a choice to stay or to go with him, he pulled her chair back and took her arm. He guided her to the stairs and they went up side by side silently.

If this was supposed to be a tour of the upstairs, it proved to be a very short one. The first door Bass came to was opened and she was pushed into the room, the door firmly shut behind Bass.

"All right, Dana. Let's have it. What's wrong now?"

Even though she could see the tautness in his body, his voice was a smooth drawl, almost as if he was bored.

Stalling for time, she fired back, "Why should anything be wrong?"

"That's what I want to know." He was beginning to lose patience with her. "I've seen more animation come from a potted plant. You've hardly said a word since we arrived home. I want to know what's bothering you."

She looked away. Home. It was his home, not hers. But she couldn't very well complain about the strangeness of everything or the attack of nerves now that she had actually gone through with the marriage. What had she really expected? An immediate declaration of love the minute they had crossed the threshold? She would have to be more patient.

Trying to change the subject, she offered, "I thought this was to be a tour of the upstairs."

He placed his hands on his hips, forcing his shirt to stretch tightly across his muscular chest. There was a moment's pause before he answered, "I thought you might like to see where you'll be sleeping."

She hadn't really looked at the room until now. It was a good-sized room with a king-size bed and dark furniture. There were loose coins on the bureau next to a cuff link box . There were several framed pictures on a dresser next to several textbook-type volumes. To confirm her sudden suspicions she went to the closet and opened the double doors. On one side of the walk-in closet were his suits, shirts, and slacks. On the other side hung the few clothes that had been in her suitcase, unpacked by the efficient Mrs. Bird.

Dana shut the doors and turned her head toward Bass. "This is your room."

"And yours," he said quietly but firmly.

She sighed, "You didn't hear a word I said earlier, did you?"

A corner of his mouth lifted in an enticing smile that weakened her resolve. "About our sleeping together? Oh, I heard you. I just didn't take it seriously."

"Well, perhaps you'd better start taking it seriously now."

He slowly came toward her and she began to back away. His eyes told her he knew her better than she knew herself. His hands rested lightly on her hips. "We're going to start this marriage the right way, Dana. If you weren't so stubborn, you would admit you want this as much as I do."

Her protests were muffled by his kiss, which was a devastating assault on her senses. The pressure of his lips parted hers, inflaming the blood in her veins and firing her desire. He was right. She did want this . . . and more. Her arms slipped around his neck as she melted against his body in an attempt to get as close as physically possible. There was a possessive warmth in his kiss that had been missing before, and she reveled in it. Who was she kidding? She was his . . . in every way possible.

Her shirt was tugged out of the waistband of her slacks as his hands caressed the bare skin underneath. Unaware of what she was doing, she began to massage his back, enjoying the feel of him under her hands. His mouth nuzzled her throat briefly before returning to her lips.

For a moment he gently pulled away from her, his eyes serious and slightly glazed with passion. Satisfied with what he read in her expression, he lifted her into his arms and carried her to his bed. He gently lowered her onto the mattress and lay down beside her.

As he toyed with a lock of her silken hair, he asked gently, “Any regrets?”

Without thinking, she murmured, “Not yet.”

He laughed softly, “Relax, darling. I won’t hurt you.”

A moment of sanity made its way into the cocoon of sensuality that enveloped her.

"Will it work, Bass? I mean between you and me. Everything has happened so fast. Did we do the right thing by getting married without knowing each other longer?"

"Are you scared it won't work out?"

Her reply was a mere whisper, "Yes."

His breath brushed lightly against her hair as he said, "Do you want it to work out?"

Again she replied, "Yes."

He lifted his head and his fingers moved up to her face, gently tracing her brow and cheekbones before moving down to her lips. "Would it help if I told you I love you?"

He smiled at her quick intake of breath. Her eyes searched his, trying to find the truth in their depths. She breathed, "If it's true."

His hands drew her gently against him, his warmth enveloping her. "At first I knew I wanted you, to make love to you. There was no doubt about that. Then I realized it was more than just lust for a beautiful body. But when I found out about J.P. and your mother, I knew I had to move fast. I knew you wouldn't agree to an affair, not after what happened between your mother and my father." While he was explaining, his hand took hold of one of hers and brought it to his chest. In a husky voice, he said, "I had to ignore your hate of my father which seemed to carry over against me."

"Why did you feel you had to hurry?"

"You were off balance with so many things happening at once . . . J.P. at the Village, my discovery of Terry," he smiled knowingly. "And your reaction to me. I had to tie you down to me before you could figure a way to leave town with Terry."

His hands moved through her hair as he rolled over to partially cover her body. "The only encouragement I had was when I held you." His smile was tender. "You didn't react like someone who felt only hate when I kissed you. It was all I had to go on but it was enough to keep me going after you. I had to let you sort out your feelings about J.P. and the past but I couldn't give you too much time in case you panicked."

With an abandon that would have shocked her if she had been capable of thinking, Dana allowed Bass to lead her along a path of sensuality to the land where lovers discover each other. She at last surrendered to him and to herself as they were both consumed by fires of passion.

Later, as if he understood her wealth of feeling, Bass gently held her, whispering soothing words of love. He brushed her hair away from her face and kissed her. "Oh

God, Dana. I love you. More than I thought I was capable of loving anyone."

Rather shyly, Dana looked up at him. "I was afraid you only wanted me. I didn't want you to make love to me because I was afraid you would be disappointed."

"Disappointed?" Bass rolled onto his back, bringing her with him, holding her tightly in his arms. "Are you crazy, woman? Why did you think I would be disappointed? Don't you realize even now how passionate you are?"

She smiled at his shocked tone. "Well, how was I supposed to know?"

He moved her away from him slightly so he could see her face. "What changed your mind?"

"You said you loved me."

He groaned. "Do you mean you've put me through all that frustration just because you thought I didn't love you? Why did you think I married you?"

She bit her lip. "Because of Terry. You wanted him to become a Ravenel so you had to take me too."

He shook his head in mock impatience. "Who can ever figure a woman's mind? Don't you think I could have gotten Terry legally without having to include his sister?" She felt him begin to grow tense. "Exactly why did you marry me, Dana?"

She raised herself on his chest and trailed a finger across his lips. Meeting his eyes squarely, she admitted, "I love you. I have for a long time."

His response was everything she could have wished for. He rolled her over, and his driving kiss pressed her against the bed. They were in danger of losing themselves in each other again when a slamming door downstairs and Terry's laugh made them realize they were not the only people in the house.

Gently, Bass released her. "We have all the time in the world, darling. Get dressed. I want to show you your new studio."

She stared at him. "My studio?"

"I had one of the outbuildings cleaned out and it is perfect for you to use as a painting studio." He pulled her off the bed and into his arms. "It will give you the chance to do something you've always wanted to do." He smiled. "Though I hope your inspiration will come during the day while I'm working. That way, we can let the nights take care of themselves."

We hope you have enjoyed this Large Print book. Other Thorndike Press or Chivers Press Large Print books are available at your library or directly from the publishers.

For more information about current and upcoming titles, please call or write, without obligation, to:

Thorndike Press
P.O. Box 159
Thorndike, Maine 04986 USA
Tel. (800) 257-5157

OR

Chivers Press Limited
Windsor Bridge Road
Bath BA2 3AX
England
Tel. (0225) 335336

All our Large Print titles are designed for easy reading, and all our books are made to last.